MAID UNDER THE MISTLETOE

A MAPLETON FAMILY SAGA NOVELLA

ANNABELLE ANDERS

To my niece, Charlotte.
Never stop reading!

CHAPTER 1

MISBEHAVING MAID

"Y ou've never looked lovelier, Miss Fairchild. Your eyes sparkle like the winter sky. Your lips glisten like the ripest of berries. The shine in your hair surely must rival all the Regent's gold."

The Honorable Miss Fairchild tittered into her handkerchief, but a gurgling noise escaped from the diminutive maid walking behind them. Anthony Crespin, Earl of Mapleton, furrowed his brows as he turned his attention to his future betrothed's companion.

Had Miss Fairchild's *maid* just rolled her eyes?

He was not mistaken. She met his backwards glance with a shrug, as though to say, *Is that the best you can do?*

"But what of my dress, my lord?" Miss Fairchild demanded his attention once again. "And my complexion?"

This time, there was no mistaking the barking noise that quickly turned into a cough.

"Is something ailing you, Charlotte?" Miss Fairchild scowled in her direction. "I do hope you aren't coming down with something. With Christmas just a few days away that would be most inconvenient."

Large eyes, with nearly as many flecks of green as blue, widened in innocence. "A ladybug landed on my nose. Ticklish little creature." The maid swiped at a most impertinent appendage. Upturned and defiant but smallish, much like its owner.

Ladybug? In late December?

"Hrmph." The genteel lady beside him studied her maid suspiciously. "You'll do well to control yourself in the future." Anthony had not noticed the shrillness of Miss Fairchild's voice before.

He tugged at his cravat, which suddenly seemed tighter than it had when he'd left Maplehurst that morning. Mindful of his manners, he offered his arm to Miss Fairchild once again.

The match between himself and Viscount Denton's eldest daughter may have been a trifle rushed, but now he had nothing left to do but actually offer for the gel.

Anthony had inherited his father's title, that of Earl of Mapleton, just over five years ago. Having recently achieved the ancient age of thirty, he'd decided the time had come to take a wife and set up a nursery.

As expected, it was what gentlemen did.

He'd originally allowed himself two to three years to view the field of eligible debutantes, but the need became urgent when two thirds of the structures within the local village burned to the ground.

And Lord Denton's estate in Hampshire conveniently bordered his own to the north. The substantial dowry, although not outlandish, would cover the cost of recovering for the fire at Bridge's End. He'd known of the honorable

Miss Fairchild for some time. The family had good connections. She maintained a spotless reputation and was not too horrible to look at. In fact, he'd managed to note that she could be rather pretty, really, when complimented and admired.

Clutching his arm possessively, Miss Fairchild leaned into him. "The sky appears as though it might snow this afternoon."

Anthony glanced upward. Not a cloud in sight. The lady was simply making conversation and so he nodded in agreement.

By Christmas, he'd be a betrothed man.

He tugged at his cravat again. When had Penrose begun knotting it so tightly? He'd have to have a word with his valet…

Hearing more muffled laughter, he glanced over his shoulder at the maid.

And again, she flashed those innocent eyes. Despite covering her hair with a simple mop cap, and wearing a frumpy grey gown, the petite young woman stirred him uncomfortably.

He determinedly faced forward and frowned. Such insubordination was quite extraordinary. He ought to be angry on behalf of Miss Fairchild. He ought to admonish the maid himself.

"And are you hoping for snow on Christmas this year?" He asked the young lady beside him. He drew in a deep breath, expecting to inhale a sweet feminine fragrance, but instead was forced to stifle his own choking sounds. Had Miss Fairchild bathed in her perfume this morning? The cloying scent of roses hung onto his senses as tightly as the wearer gripped his arm.

"Of course not, my lord! If it snows, our guests might have difficulty travelling to the Christmas Ball." She paused meaningfully. "And they might miss the announcement."

Damn, but the temperature had risen since they'd stepped outside ten minutes ago. He could not remember the last time it had been so warm around the holidays.

She had the right of it, for certain. He fully intended for her father to make the announcement at the Christmas Ball.

Miss Fairchild's parents, Lord and Lady Denton, were hosting several people for the holidays. Lofty guests who all had high expectations for Miss Fairchild. He was saved from making any comment when approaching voices carried along the garden path.

He recognized Mr. and Mrs. Smythe, one of Miss Fairchild's married cousins and her husband, and Lord and Lady Pritchard. His own younger brother and sister walked with them as well. Likely, Daphne was doing her best to allow him some privacy with Miss Fairchild. His younger sister was all too aware of his responsibilities and whenever possible, did what she could to assist him in meeting them. She could be as annoying at times, as she could be sweet.

Michael was all of seven and twenty, still enjoying the exploits of young bachelorhood, and Daphne was only five years younger than Michael. Their mother remained at home, abed. She'd not come out of her bedchamber since their father's passing.

Miss Fairchild released his arm in order to join them, leaving Anthony standing alone with her maid.

Was this what marriage to her would be like?

"More like lapis, after it has dried and been ground up." The small woman beside him offered with a smirk.

"Excuse me?" Maids did not have discussions with their mistress's escorts.

"A more apt description for her eyes." She grinned. "Although the flower is a brilliant color while alive, the vivid hue is lost shorty after it's picked." At his frown, she elaborated. "Not at all like a bright winter sky."

Again, that sensation that he would like to reprimand this defiant servant… if only he did not find a part of himself agreeing with her. She was correct about both, he conceded, recalling the plant to which she referred, and how disappointed one became as it dried out.

"You oughtn't." He uttered instead.

She sighed heavily and he could not help to notice how the rise and fall of her breasts topped off what he guessed must be a perfect hourglass figure.

He pulled his gaze back to her face quickly. A gentleman did not ogle his intended's maid.

"Oh, believe me, I know." She sighed again and watched Miss Fairchild fawn over the other guests. "It's just too easy sometimes."

He studied her skeptically. He did not remember seeing her with Miss Fairchild before. In fact, he remembered quite distinctly that a heavy-set woman had accompanied them on their last outing.

"Have you only recently entered service?" Oddly enough, he didn't want the girl to bring trouble upon herself. But for the luck of birth, his own sister might have fallen into such a position.

She grimaced as she met his stare. "This is my fourth position."

He raised his brows.

"In three months."

Ahh…

Well, he could not feign surprise.

~

CHARLOTTE DRAKE KNEW she was treading on thin ice again. Not only by pointing out that her mistress's eyes resembled a faded flower, but by addressing Lord Mapleton in the first place.

Oliver would throttle her if she got sacked again. As it was, her brother and his wife, Betsy, barely had enough room to accommodate their own family. They certainly didn't have additional provisions to care for her.

She would never forget her brother's horrified expression when she'd shown up on his doorstep thirteen weeks ago. They'd expected she would dwell with father for another decade or two, possibly three, at the vicarage. Not one person could have predicted his untimely death. He'd only been fifty-three, for heaven's sake! It was circumstances such as these that had Charlotte questioning God's judgment at times.

Especially his taking her mother's life upon her own birth.

Dismissing the painful thought, her mind wandered.

She should have married Jonathan Birch when he'd offered four years ago. Surely being a wife could not have been worse than catering to the demands of Miss Susan Fairchild.

She shrugged off her musings, all too aware that Lord Mapleton watched her warily.

"Are you going to make and offer then?" Charlotte could not help but ask. It was all Lady Denton and Miss Fairchild had been talking about since Charlotte took up her post this week.

Again, Lord Mapleton raised his brows at her words. She eyed their fullness, the dark brown color, and their finely shaped appearance. Just beneath the tall hat perched atop his person, dark blond hairs framed his perfectly sized head. As far as gentlemen went, he really was one of the finer looking ones. Miss Fairchild could do much worse, that was for certain.

Any of the husbands of her former employers caused Lord Mapleton to shine in comparison. And not just in looks, either.

In character… She had a sense about such things.

She'd sensed that Mr. Merkle was trouble at the onset of that particular post.

A tremor of disgust ran through her at the memory of her last employer's hands 'accidentally' brushing across the tops of her breasts. And Mrs. Merkle had shown no sympathy whatsoever. In fact, she'd blamed Charlotte for her husband's nefarious behavior.

"Did you seriously take it upon yourself to ask me if I was going to propose to your mistress, Miss…?"

"Drake." She supplied, holding out her hand. "Charlotte Drake."

Again, with those eyebrows of his. But oh, dear. The nearby group silenced as they stared back at them. Of course, a servant did not offer her hand to a lord!

Class distinction. Class differences. She'd experienced it all of her life, with her father's parishioners. How different it was to now endure the subtle and not so subtle differences from an even less advantageous perspective.

She dropped her hand and began reaching into the

pockets of her coat. "I had one somewhere, my lord." She spoke in her most obsequious voice while withdrawing a handkerchief. She handed it to Lord Mapleton who then slowly took it. Although he looked startled, he stuffed it into his pocket without contradicting her.

Ah, she'd known he must be something of a good person.

"Thank you, Miss Drake."

And then he bowed.

What was he doing?

He failed to comprehend the huge blunder he was making until too late. This time he was the one forced to recover. Fumbling back into his pockets, he withdrew the handkerchief once again and then dropped it to the ground. He then bent the rest of the way down and scooped it up.

Charlotte slid a sideways glance at the new arrivals. Had they noticed? One of the older women narrowed her eyes in their direction. Did the woman think Charlotte was flirting with an earl? Instead of allowing her inclination to return the lady's scowl, Charlotte dropped her gaze submissively.

She could have choked on a sob in that moment, because God help her, she didn't know if she could do this.

Miss Fairchild marched over. "Go inside, Drake. And advise my mother that I no longer have need of a chaperone." Miss Fairchild ordered. "I no longer have need of *you*."

Oh dear!

The older woman who'd seemed suspicious made a few tsking sounds but the younger looking women gave her a sympathetic smile. She seemed familiar, somehow.

Blondish hair. Friendly eyes. Oh, but she must be Lord Mapleton's sister. And the man beside her was obviously his brother. They all exhibited the unmistakable aristocratic demeanor, but not in the same way as other members of the upper class she'd met. Their expressive eyes lacked the arrogance of the likes of the Fairchilds, the Merkles and the Smythes.

"Yes Miss Fairchild." She uttered the expected words, and then catching herself, curtsied quickly before turning for the house.

"Miss Drake." It was the earl's voice which halted her. "Your handkerchief."

Keeping her head down, she scrambled back and swiped it from his hand. Only when she had returned to Miss Fairchild's chamber did she realize he'd given her one of his own.

The small cloth had obviously been laundered numerous times, as the embroidered designs had long since faded. Delicate leaves were sewn around the monogram. Far more than would have been considered adequate.

Someone had made the handkerchief specially for him, Charlotte surmised. She wondered if it had been his sister, or his mother, or some other special lady.

Stuffing into her pocket, she made a mental note to herself to return it.

"WHAT DID HE SAY TO YOU?" Two hours later, Charlotte endured Susan Fairchild's inquisition as she assisted the girl out of her day dress.

She had already received a sound scolding from the housekeeper. Mrs. Gibson had warned her that if she spoke up without being asked one more time, Lady Denton would send Charlotte away immediately and without a reference.

"I caught you speaking with him." The girl's voice was muffled by the material draping over her face. "I demand you tell me what he said."

So, Susan was not perhaps so very certain of Lord Mapleton's intent. Charlotte thought quickly of anything to reassure her. "He asked me if I thought you would have him." It was a lie but... a harmless one. One that might improve Charlotte's own position in that moment. "He asked... um, if you were excited at the prospect of becoming Countess, um... Mapleton."

Susan's head emerged, a satisfied expression on her face. Charlotte's fabrication had accomplished exactly what she'd hoped.

"He did? I wondered if that was what he was saying. What else would an earl have to discuss with a servant? And what did you tell him?"

"What would you have had me tell him?" She countered. For until today Charlotte had only heard talk of his estate and his money and how all the debutantes this spring would be most jealous that Miss Fairchild landed one of England's most sought-after gentlemen.

Susan bit her lip. "I suppose I would have you tell him that, of course, I would accept him. Why ever would I not? He is an earl! I shall become Lady Mapleton."

Charlotte could almost feel sorry for these nobs. They married for reasons other than love and then sought pleasure elsewhere. "I told him you found him utterly handsome and kind—that you thought he had the warmest eyes and lovely hair. I told him you could hardly wait to be caught under the mistletoe..." Had she gone too far?

But even this spoiled young woman was not immune to

Lord Mapleton's dashing good looks. She stared at herself in the mirror with a dreamy smile.

"I shall be a countess! You'll have to address me as 'my lady' then, you know."

Or perhaps Susan Fairchild was less immune to his other… assets.

Charlotte's mistress then climbed into her gigantic bed and pushed her feet under the covers. "Steam my rose-colored gown for dinner. And I want my satin slippers brushed. Awaken me in two hours. I'll have a bath then. And be quiet about filling it while I rest." And then she swept the curtain closed in dismissal.

Charlotte hated being a servant.

CHAPTER 2

SECOND THOUGHTS

"*B*etter you than me, that's all I can say." Anthony's brother, Michael, dropped his hat on the bench beside him in the carriage. "Don't get me wrong, I stand by your decision whole-heartedly. But if you aren't certain you want to live with the woman for the remainder of your days, perhaps you ought to duck out. Go to London after the holidays and see if you can find a more palatable chit."

"He's as good as declared himself." This from Daphne. She'd been even more quiet than usual throughout the tea their hosts had served. "If he fails to come up to snuff, he'll gain a reputation for being something of a scoundrel."

"Better than live out his days regretting the leg shackle." Michael's irreverence only served to remind Anthony of his own misgivings. Anthony held his own hat on his lap, in gloved hands as the carriage rocked into motion, drawing them away from his neighbor's estate.

Would he regret marrying Miss Fairchild? He hadn't noticed any serious doubts until this afternoon.

"Miss Fairchild was most unkind to her companion."

Daphne's words reminded him of the moment these doubts had appeared. "I understand the girl lost her father recently."

"She cannot have been raised in service." He stared outside at the passing scenery as he commented. Anthony had made sure to be extra attentive to Miss Fairchild for the remainder of the visit. Perhaps she would forget her companion's unfortunate behavior. Good God, and his own! He'd nearly bowed to the girl! A servant, for heaven's sake.

She'd reached out her hand for him to take.

To an earl!

Impudent wench.

Miss Charlotte Drake deserved to be sacked and yet... their easy interaction had knocked him off his guard... he'd wanted to protect her for some reason. A rare intelligence lurked behind her gaze.

"Miss Frye said her brother recommended Miss Drake to Lord Denton. Vicar Frye acted as curate for her father years ago." Anthony had known Vicar Frye for as long as he could remember. The man lived up to his calling.

"Miss Drake is a vicar's daughter?" So, he was correct in his assumption that she'd not been raised or trained for her current vocation. Miss Drake's inappropriate behavior made some sense then. She'd been educated at some point. If Anthony were to take a guess, he'd hazard she'd been a bit spoiled.

"She's not going to last a week." Daphne announced with a grimace. "She's far too outspoken, but even worse, far too pretty."

He could not dispute either of his sister's assertions.

"I couldn't tell if her eyes were green or blue." Daphne continued. "Beautiful, she truly is beautiful. I wonder what color her hair is. I couldn't quite make it out beneath her mob cap." His sister settled into the seat comfortably beside him.

"Her eyes are blue, with green flecks." He provided. And since her brows are blond, "I'd wager her hair is blond."

Silence met his response.

"What color are Miss Fairchild's eyes?" His sister attempted to sound nonchalant as she asked the question, but Anthony was all too aware that even his younger brother paid close attention for his answer.

Miss Fairchild's eyes were barely blue. Miss Drake had had the right of it. "Blue."

Michael raised his brows at the answer and Daphne sighed.

"Did you think I'd not know the color of my intended's eyes?"

"Miss Fairchild is not your intended yet." Michael pointed out.

"But for all intents and purposes, she is." This was not the first time these two had bickered that morning. Through most of their childhoods, Anthony had felt like something of a referee.

"What color is Miss Fairchild's hair?" Michael would return to this line of questioning.

"Blondish brown." Anthony surmised. A rather unremarkable color all around. "Now if you both are done with your inquisition––"

"Dull brown." Michael interjected. "Her eyes are dull blue, her hair a dull brown and her face, a very dull face. It seems, my dear brother, that you have chosen a woman for her very dullness in particular."

"She will not be boring." Daphne, dearest Daphne jumped to Miss Fairchild's defense. "She will do her best to make everyone around her quite miserable."

"Daph!" Anthony turned toward her. "You'll do well to keep such comments to yourself in the future."

Of course, his sister had an opinion. Since their mother had taken to her chamber, Daphne had taken over the running of the household. She would relinquish that duty to his future wife.

To Miss Fairchild.

"You are going to offer for her tomorrow?" Michael looked serious for the first time since they'd climbed into the carriage.

Anthony's infernal cravat all but strangled him. Good God, he was going to have to speak with Penrose about his unbearably tight knots!

"Perhaps I'll wait another day. Propose on Christmas Eve. I will take her driving tomorrow––into the village. I've a few last-minute Christmas gifts to purchase."

"So you will delay. Effective tactic, brother. But it won't work forever."

Younger siblings could be more annoying than a horse-hair sweater on a humid day.

"You'll be wise to keep quiet today." Susan advised Charlotte while preening at the looking glass. "I do wish Mama didn't insist you ride along. It's not as though we're in

London. A chaperone ought not be necessary for an innocent drive into the village."

Charlotte had no choice but to accompany the courting couple once again this afternoon. She must, however, keep herself from commenting upon the Earl's obviously contrived compliments and simply be thankful for the chance to venture out. She'd already gotten a glimpse of the lovely vehicle. The ride would be a treat alone. A chilly one, but a treat, nonetheless.

As she tugged her right glove over her hand, her pinky slipped out the end of the fingertip. She'd been meaning to mend it, but all her sewing energies had been put to work repairing the hems on three of Miss Fairchild's gowns.

She never would have thought she'd miss the luxury of sewing her own garments.

Oh, Papa!

Unwittingly, Charlotte found herself blinking hard. It hadn't been so very long ago since she'd been her own mistress and her time had been her own. Her greatest worry had been escaping church services without being held up by the local gossips. How naïve and foolish she had been!

Pushing the maudlin memories away, she followed Miss Fairchild out of her chamber. When they reached the balustrade, Charlotte nearly plowed the other girl over when she stopped dramatically and posed for inspection. Lord Mapleton stood below, with his head tilted upward and his hat in hand.

Like any good suitor, he anxiously awaited Miss Fairchild's appearance——or appeared to be doing so, anyhow.

Because his gaze did not trail after the young lady of the house. No, it landed upon Charlotte.

No! No! No! Whatever was he thinking? Was it his intent to make her life miserable?

Charlotte scowled down at him and lowered her own gaze to her hands. It was just the sort of thing Lady Denton would notice.

"I hope I haven't kept you waiting overly long." Susan called down in a treacle-sweet voice, feigning regret. All three of them knew for a fact that he'd arrived forty minutes earlier. And he likely knew as well as they, that Miss Fairchild had been dressed and ready but insisted upon making him wait.

"Time is of no matter when you are the prize, Miss Fairchild."

Charlotte required all of her resolve not to roll her eyes heavenward. Did he not realize how ridiculous these compliments sounded?

The object of his gibberish sighed dreamily and descended the steps with more haughtiness that a queen. When Charlotte dared to glance his way again, the blighter winked—yes, he winked—at *her*! He'd known the compliment was rubbish.

Oh, but this was not good at all! Because Charlotte's lips twitched back at him.

He was an earl—an aristocrat. And she ...

Although she'd once been a gentleman's daughter. She was now a servant.

Not that she lacked intelligence, or manners. In truth, she knew herself to be just as good as Miss Susan Fairchild —excepting, of course, the twist of fate that landed Charlotte with a vicar for a father, and Miss Fairchild, a viscount.

Many believed the classes within society to have been ordained by God. This opinion had never failed to derive a hearty scoff from Charlotte's father. Such a God would be cruel indeed. To give every human a brain, needs and desires, and then to only allow a select few to benefit from all the world had to offer would have been a mean irony, indeed.

Having spent time in service now, albeit only a few months, she'd come to be friends with a few of her fellow servants. They were not emotionless beings without hopes, dreams and fears.

She'd known all of this logically, of course, but now she knew it with her *heart.*

Lately, she wished that she didn't--know better, that was. Because if she hadn't been taught otherwise by her father, she might not mind so very much trailing behind another human being in subjective humility. She might not mind the insults and degrading comments or being allotted such a lowering place in society.

Her mind argued back that she would still mind all of it. Something to contemplate later, when she wasn't under the scrutiny of her new employers.

Lady Denton descended the stairs behind them. "You are a lucky fellow indeed, my lord! Just last night Lord Creighton expressed the wish to take my darling daughter for a drive. I told him you'd reserved her this afternoon, of course, but he promised he'd try another day."

"Mama!" Susan protested half-heartedly.

"How right you are, my lady." He did not miss a beat, this one. Charlotte pinched her lips together tightly and assisted Susan with the elaborate bonnet she'd chosen to wear that day.

"We've yet to see any snow, my lord." Her young mistress exhibited a brilliant aptitude for meaningless conversation.

Charlotte refrained from sighing heavily. She hated talk of the weather when there were so many other topics to discuss, topics that mattered. There were plenty of subjects where one might express an opinion and then defend it with logic and reason, and then allow one's companion to do the same. And yet she could not keep her gaze from shifting to the window. Snow had covered the ground last year at Christmas time. She and Papa had made a snowman and then had a snow war.

"Another beautiful day indeed." The blighter directed his response toward Miss Fairchild, but Charlotte felt his gaze fall upon herself. "Are you ladies ready then?"

Ladies?

Again, Charlotte wondered, *Is he trying to get me sacked?*

"Mama is not coming with us." Luckily, Miss Fairchild failed to comprehend his faux pas.

Gentlemen did not refer to a servant as a lady.

"Ah." Clearing his throat, he pointed his gaze toward a most benign watercolor hanging on the wall. "Such a shame." And then seemingly recovered, he offered his arm to Miss Fairchild and led her outside.

Crisp air. Hazy blue sky. And the open landau was even prettier up close.

"Hand me my parasol, Drake. Did you forget it again? Fetch it now and make haste. We haven't all day." The girl barked her demand without so much as a glance in Charlotte's direction. "I must be careful of the sun, you know." Susan fluttered barely-there eyelashes in the direction of Lord Mapleton.

Just ten minutes earlier the girl had insisted she would not require a parasol today. With her new resolve to not get herself fired, Charlotte bit back a caustic retort and dashed back inside. As she climbed the stairs, muttering to herself, she nearly ran down Lady Denton.

"Excuse me, ma'am. My lady, I mean." She mumbled as she went to pass.

But a tight grasp kept her from going any farther. "My husband hired you, gel, but I can fire you any time I wish. Step carefully, now." And she just as quickly dropped her hand, leaving a stunned Charlotte in her wake.

Lady Denton had obviously noticed Lord Mapleton's misplaced attentions. And, oh dear, she'd possibly heard him address Charlotte—*the maid*—as a lady, along with her daughter. The Viscountess was clearly not as oblivious as her daughter.

Eyes down, Charlotte scampered up the stairs, retrieved the parasol and reluctantly headed back outside.

Miss Fairchild had arranged herself most elegantly on the bench in the open vehicle, but Lord Mapleton waited nearby, supposedly to assist her up as well.

Which ought to be innocent enough.

If only he would stop watching her!

"Miss Drake," he extended one hand. Thinking quickly, Charlotte slapped the closed end of the parasol into it.

"You will kindly hand this to Miss Fairchild?" And then she curtsied.

CHAPTER 3

PURCHASING GIFTS

The sting on his hand reminded Anthony that this lady, this young woman, *a servant*, did not wish his attention, and most definitely did not want his kindness.

He ought to kick himself for his bumbling behavior already this morning. Miss Drake was Miss *Fairchild's companion*, he reminded himself for the umpteenth time since meeting her.

With an expression of impassivity he didn't feel, he stood behind the unsettling young woman as she lifted her foot to climb up. She was half a head shorter than Miss Fairchild but if she wished to do this herself, who was he to deny her the accomplishment?

One attempt. Fail.

Another.

Another yet.

Feeling more awkward than he had in over a decade, Anthony stepped forward only for her to motion him to back up. Servant or not, did the woman not realize any gentleman would not stand by while a lady, a girl, *a woman*, for *God's sake*, struggled to climb into a vehicle?

Dash it all! He reached out, planted his hands on her waist and lifted her up and onto the conveyance.

He did not expect the bolt of awareness that shot through him upon touching her. Warmth. Tingling consciousness. His hands had nearly encircled her waist and she'd weighed little more than a child. But she most definitely had not affected him like a child. As he'd lifted her, nothing in the world could have prevented his gaze from focusing on her round hips and derriere. And when she steadied herself before climbing on, a whiff of sweet feminine essence threatened to hold him captive.

Time stood still until Miss Fairchild's voice jerked him out of his stupor.

"Did you forget something, my lord?" Mild irritation laced her voice moving him to climb aboard to join them.

What on earth was the matter with him?

Miss Drake sat in the subservient position with her back to the horses and Miss Fairchild forward facing. Still dazed from the strange effect Miss Drake evoked, he swallowed hard and took his place beside his companion for the day. Then he looked anywhere but at the young woman directly in front of him.

"You are such a *man*, Mapleton." A delicate fan landed upon his chest as Miss Fairchild tapped him flirtatiously. "To have put off your purchases until the last minute. Mother and I did most of our shopping in London during the little season."

"It's wonderful the shops have reopened already. It hasn't been that long since the fire." Miss Drake inserted.

"Pftt." Miss Fairchild scoffed. "I hope you find something of value, my lord. The local goods fail miserably in comparison to what can be found in the windows alone, on Oxford Street."

"I'm confident I'll find something in Mr. Blanchard's inventory to satisfy my needs." In fact, he made it a point to support the local shops with his patronage whenever possible. Not everyone was fortunate enough to travel to London to purchase their necessities. And it was those same people who provided the comforts for the more affluent members in the area. Which was why he'd invested so heavily in rebuilding the village as quickly as possible.

Anthony tilted his head awkwardly in order to avoid losing an eye to the parasol Miss Fairchild swirled recklessly upon her shoulder.

"I'm horrible at shopping," he admitted. "How is a gentleman to know what the ladies in his life wish for?" It was the reason he always grappled at the last moment. His mother had everything she could possibly want, except for his father, of course. An all too familiar emptiness passed through him at the thought. Daphne was even more difficult to please. She'd prefer to give all the sum of her worldly possessions to the poor. Another point of contention between her and Michael.

Anthony had purchased a walking cane for Michael as something of a joke. His brother had taken great pains to give Anthony grief last spring, when he'd met up with him at White's with one in hand.

The cane was a beauty, with an ivory handle and a lion's head carved into the stick. Even Michael couldn't help but appreciate such a find.

"Jewelry is always welcome." Miss Fairchild fluttered her lashes in his direction. "Or anything that costs a pretty penny, for that matter."

"Duly noted." He smiled, but her suggestion grated. It shouldn't, as future gifts he'd procure for his wife would be paid for with her dowry, partially anyhow.

"For whom have you yet to acquire a gift, my lord?"

Miss Drake's voice dragged his gaze to stare across the conveyance at her.

She held it with her own startlingly lovely blue eyes, making him feel as though he was caught underwater. As though the world around them ceased to exist.

"I've yet to find anything for my mother," he confessed. "Or Lady Daphne, my sister."

Tiny fingers tapped the bottom of the most darling chin. "Hmm..." She seemed to be contemplating a matter of great import. As she did so, he noticed that the tip of her pinky finger protruded from a tear in her well-worn gloves.

And then she asked, "What three words would you use to describe your sister?"

Hmm. "Intrepid. Practical. Yet...romantic." He shrugged at the descriptors which seemingly made no sense but were most assuredly accurate.

"I think perhaps a muff. One that's fabulously soft and ridiculously feminine. When she ventures into the cold later this winter, she'll have something practical to wear but it shall also have the added value of reminding her of her thoughtful and caring brother."

He did care for Daphne. Very much.

In that moment, he wondered at her extraordinary perception for the perfect gift.

"And your mother?" Miss Drake wasted no time doubting her first suggestion.

Defining his mother was a little more difficult. Descriptors he'd use now being quite different than what they would have been before his father's passing.

"Sad." The word left his mouth before he could stop it. "But content. And… delicate." His mother had once been an older version of his sister. Melancholy embraced him whenever he considered the woman she had been before…

Astute eyes narrowed at him thoughtfully. They held a little sympathy but mostly the countenance of a person who listened. A person who listened and actually contemplated what he'd said—and even what he'd not said.

"A painting. Watercolors, I think. A dreamy landscape." And then she smiled.

Again, her suggestion rattled him.

"Do me, my lord! What three words would you use to describe me? And then Charlotte can help you pick out the perfect gift!"

For some odd reason, Anthony had not had any difficulty in deciding upon a gift for Miss Fairchild. He'd bought her an ornate looking fan. Ostentatious in its design, it would capture her interest for all of one minute. He'd intended to present it to her on Christmas day, which would be socially acceptable, as she'd be his fiancé by then.

But for now, he sat gazing into Miss Drake's azure colored eyes as though he had not a care elsewhere. Reluctantly, he shifted and turned so that he could pretend interest in the lady he intended to ask to be his wife.

What three words would best describe Miss Fairchild?

"Lovely." The word flowed all too easily off his tongue.

In truth, he found her pretty in the most abstract fashion. "Discerning." Picky to a fault. He now realized he did not appreciate the manner in which she addressed her father's servants. "And..." He struggled as he searched for another complimentary adjective. *Think Anthony. Think.*

"And?" Miss Fairchild prodded.

"And..." The abundance of lace on her dress distracted him for a moment. "Fashionable."

She smiled in satisfaction and turned to look across the small space at Miss Drake. "You cannot speak aloud what Lord Mapleton ought to buy me, because then it would not be a surprise! No, you must assist him once we've arrived at the shops!" She seemed all too happy to arrange the excursion.

Alarm bells rang in Anthony's brain. Not because of any concern that Miss Fairchild wouldn't approve of any gift he presented to her, but because, by God, he wanted nothing more than to spend the afternoon *alone with Miss Drake.*

The companion.

Miss Fairchild's companion.

"And what of Lord Mapleton, Drake?" Miss Fairchild pinned her stare upon her maid. "What would make the perfect gift for the earl?"

Anthony couldn't help but want to know her answer. Not that he wanted a gift from Miss Fairchild, or any gift at all, but he found himself quite delighted with Miss Drake's creative method for gift giving.

He found himself delighted with Miss Drake, all in all.

"What three words would you use to describe his lordship?" She turned the question back at her mistress.

What words would Miss Fairchild come up with, indeed?

The lady beside him frowned. "Three words?"

"That best describe Lord Mapleton." Miss Drake nodded.

"Ah…" Now it was Miss Fairchild's turn to falter. "Handsome." An appropriate answer even if Anthony did not completely agree with her assessment. His appearance, he considered for the most part, to be passable.

"Titled." True enough. He could hardly wait to hear her third adjective.

"And well-off." This surprised him. It shouldn't, he certainly wasn't a pauper. But most of his wealth was tied up in estate improvements, thus the need to marry…

And in that moment, the coldhearted manner for which he'd chosen his future wife and the no-nonsense approach behind her likely acceptance, became all too crystal. And strikingly clear.

As a younger man he'd hoped for love. Perhaps it had been an abstract dream of his. But he'd failed to find it in any suitable lady. Or any lady at all, for that matter.

And so, he'd resorted to the way things were done.

"I've already purchased a gift for Lord Mapleton, Charlotte, but do tell me what you think he would want." Miss Fairchild slid a sideways glance in his direction, as though she was finding great amusement with this game.

Miss Drake turned and studied him intently. As though paralyzed, he couldn't look away to save his life. Something visceral connected them. He couldn't shake the feeling that she was looking into his mind and heart and reading him easier than she'd read any book.

"I would not purchase a gift for Lord Mapleton." She surprised them both for only a moment before adding. "He seems the sort who would far more appreciate a labor of love." And then she tapped her chin thoughtfully three more times. "I'd either knit him a scarf so that he'd think of me whenever he used it to keep the cold out or… give him one of my lockets, and in it a few strands of my hair."

All of the air whooshed out of his lungs making him barely aware of the tsking sounds coming from Miss Fairchild. "Absurd, Charlotte! Absolutely absurd! As if an earl would want a strand of hair in an old locket!"

But all Anthony could think was how incredibly delightful such a gift would be…with a swirl of blond hair enclosed.

THE MORE CHARLOTTE came to know of Lord Mapleton, the greater she esteemed him. The earl not only loved his sister, he liked her. And he physically ached for his mother.

Had his mother embroidered the handkerchief he'd inadvertently handed her the day before? Or had his sister?

Sensing the warmth of his familial relationships, she couldn't help but compare the cooler one she shared with her own brother. Oliver loved her. She had no doubt of that. But he'd never *liked* her. He'd told her on more than one occasion that he disapproved of the manner in which she spent her time. Young ladies should not read, conduct experiments or explore out of doors when other tasks needed finishing inside the home. "Such activities only lead to trouble," he'd told her. She ought to be baking, sewing, washing clothes and undertaking other such feminine pursuits. He'd quite disapproved of the fact that his father employed a housekeeper when Charlotte could just as easily have performed the requisite tasks to maintain their small household.

And she talked too much. Oh, yes. Throughout her childhood, Oliver had complained on a daily basis that she talked too much.

Charlotte glanced at the passing scenery. If her life had not been turned upside down and she'd still been living with her father, the last few warm days would have been spent exploring the winter forest, enjoying the cool sunlight. Perhaps she would be searching for the perfect gift to give her papa for Christmas.

Had Oliver been correct in his opinion of her? Would she have experienced less difficulties now if she'd not been allowed the liberties she had? As it was, the prospect of spending the remainder of her life in service was nearly enough to catapult her into a world of despair.

Charlotte grimaced at her self-indulgent thoughts.

She would not trade who she was for anything but she was going to have to rely upon her wits and imagination in this new environment. She needed to stop allowing herself these incessant bouts of self-pity. Instead she would keep a watchful eye out for traps and pitfalls that could have her fall to an even lower existence.

There were worse things, she knew, than being a lady's maid.

She tensed as the horses slowed to a stop in front of one of the newly rebuilt village shops. A few of the smaller structures remained in charred ruins but much of the debris was long gone and new construction was taking shape nicely. Charlotte had heard all about the fire that nearly put an end to the village forever but hadn't been in the area when it occurred. A tremor ran through her as she imagined flames claiming an entire village.

Mrs. Gibson, the Denton's housekeeper, had told her it was thanks to Lord Mapleton that the village wouldn't sit idle for the winter. He must be a powerful landowner, indeed.

A *caring* and powerful one.

When he'd lifted her onto the vehicle, Charlotte had nearly swooned.

Swooned! A word she'd never considered before in relation to her own state of being.

It was just that he'd lifted her so effortlessly. His clean male scent reminded her of another time in her life, of an elegant library her father had once taken her to visit. The earl had smelled of leather and wood, but something spicy too.

And she'd enjoyed the sensation of being considered and protected. It was nice not to struggle against the onerous height of the carriage.

Other men had touched her before, and she'd experienced a most opposite sort of reaction. She'd not liked being touched without permission.

But Lord Mapleton… A shiver danced down her spine.

She'd best not allow him to assist her to the ground. No. She'd hop off at her own volition. Land on her own two perfectly useful feet.

And so, before he or Miss Fairchild could rise, Charlotte shot off the bench. She practically threw herself out of the vehicle.

Oh, dear, they had been two perfectly useful feet when she'd first climbed on. Upon landing, she realized her knees had turned decidedly weak.

But she did not fall. No. Sheer willpower drove her to steady herself and wait patiently while the other two occupants descended in a much more graceful fashion. Lord Mapleton glanced at her curiously, but Miss Fairchild's face remained blank.

"I'll wait in the pastry shop while Drake assists you with my gift."

Miss Fairchild could not be serious. Could she? And yet she was gesturing across the road.

"Oh, but Miss Fairchild, your mother will have connniptions if I leave you alone. I couldn't..." But Miss Fairchild dismissed Charlotte's concerns.

"You'll only be a moment. It's not as though I'll be far away." And without another word Miss Fairchild lifted her chin stubbornly and then stepped into the road. Lord Mapleton, appearing equally chagrined as Charlotte felt, dashed after Miss Fairchild leaving Charlotte to take in her surrounding alone.

The haberdasher, dressmaker and linen shop existed together as one storefront and exhibited some of its more fashionable items in the modern window displays. Blanchard's Mercantile offered variety as well as convenience. In addition to ladies' apparel and accessories, they boasted men's apparel, small furnishings, candles, and scents.

But what could Charlotte do? If she were to follow Miss Fairchild to the pastry shop, she'd be defying her mistress' wishes out right. And yet, if Lady Denton discovered she'd left Susan alone, even for just a few minutes... Charlotte did not wish to dwell upon such a scenario.

She bit her bottom lip and folded her arms in front of her as Lord Mapleton disappeared with Miss Fairchild into the pastry shop. After just a few moments he reappeared, dashed across the road once again, and offered Charlotte his arm.

She should not take it. She should follow behind him. Shouldn't she?

But her hand felt safe and natural in the crook of his elbow. And this close she could inhale his scent deeply. The desire to swoon assaulted her again but she shook it off. *He's an earl, Charlotte. And you are a mere servant!*

The two of them stepped into the store to the clanging of bells cleverly placed so that they would not fail to draw the shopkeeper's attention.

"My dear Lord Mapleton!" An elderly man with rolled up shirtsleeves greeted her escort warmly. "Making purchases for this lovely lady today?"

"Oh but…" Her coat covered her drab gown, if not her unflattering mob cap. Of course, she would be mistaken for a lady, hanging upon the earl's arm as she was.

"I am indeed, Mr. Blanchard. And a few other purchases I've put off too long."

The owner smiled in Charlotte's direction. "He does this every year. At least he's brought help this time. Last Christmas he required the opinions of at least three of my other customers before settling upon gifts for his mother and sister. I've no doubt Lady Mapleton and Lady Daphne appreciate the effort His Lordship puts forth each year."

Charlotte couldn't help laughing at this. He'd not been lying then, when he admitted he had difficulty making such purchases. After exchanging a few vague pleasantries, Charlotte extracted herself from the earl's side. She explored the aisles and eavesdropped, while he discussed the ongoing village reconstruction with the merchant.

Since no muffs appeared to be stocked, Charlotte settled

upon a periwinkle-colored scarf made of the softest yarn she'd ever touched for Lady Daphne. His mother's gift required a little more contemplation. The prints on hand were all wrong, and so she turned to a display of various fabrics. Someone had made an elegant shawl of a fine gossamer lace. The gold and ivory tones conjured a warmth Charlotte knew it would not provide, but any mother would treasure something so extravagantly beautiful from her son.

"You think Miss Fairchild would appreciate a shawl?" Her escort's drawling voice surprised her from behind.

"For your mother." She lifted the finely crafted wrap from the display and presented it to him with a flourish. "The prints here, though lovely, are not at all what I had in mind." And then she handed him the scarf. "Mr. Blanchard seems to be out of muffs for the season."

He examined the items, turning them over in his hands carefully before nodding his approval. She knew he would like them. Even though they'd barely met she'd known what his taste would be. He appreciated quality, she could tell by his clothing, but he was not interested in the latest fashions. Although, she amended her assessment, he also took enjoyment when it was in his grasp. Why else would he arrive in an open carriage for their short drive into Bridge's End?

Charlotte wondered again at the odd sense that she'd known him much longer. Something in the manner he smiled at her. Or rather perhaps, that she could not help but to smile back.

When he finally glanced back up at her a spark of mischief lit his eyes. "But you have forgotten your task. Show me to the appropriate gift for Miss Fairchild."

Charlotte bit her lip. She'd known precisely what she would have him purchase for her charge all along...

Without stopping to consider the wisdom of her actions, she padded toward the counter displaying scents. She required no time at all to locate the one she had in mind.

Roses. Even more cloying than the perfume her mistress normally wore.

As he opened the vial and sniffed, Lord Mapleton frowned. "I have to admit to being disappointed..."

"It's strong." She paused. "So strong that you'll always know when she's approaching." And then she could not help but add, "As will her maid."

He lifted the bottle to his face and inhaled with a grimace. She'd gone too far this time.

But then he nodded sagely. "The perfect gift." And he caught her gaze with his.

And held it.

What did he see when he studied her so intently? What was he thinking? Was he imagining what it would feel like to press his lips against hers? Charlotte's breath caught. Did he feel that same pull? The one that nearly caused her to sway into him and bury her face in his neckcloth?

Charlotte reached into her pocket. "You gave this to me by mistake." It was the handkerchief with faded embroidery.

Staring at it silently, he reached out and placed his hand in hers. As his fingers curled around the fabric, they grazed her palm, in no hurry to break the momentary connection. "Thank you." His voice sounded gruffer than normal.

But then he shook his head, as though shaking her out of his thoughts. "You'll want to join Miss Fairchild now. She oughtn't be alone so long." A tight smile. "I wouldn't want there to be any trouble."

He understood her plight. Of course, he would.

Charlotte nodded and without so much as glancing at him, weaved her way out of the store and across the street.

And just in the nick of time.

CHAPTER 4

TURMOIL

"Get off! Go away!" Miss Fairchild stood outside the pastry shop with her hands in the air, as a medium sized mutt jumped enthusiastically at her skirts. Her eyes pleaded for assistance when she caught sight of Charlotte, who made a mad dash across the road. "He's going to bite me! Drake, get him off me!"

"Down boy!" Charlotte ordered the excited pup, who's tail wagged exuberantly at such a fun game. "He only wants your meat pie." She tried to reassure Miss Fairchild who was shaking and near tears.

Charlotte bent down and wrapped her arms around a scruffy and malodorous neck. "You need a bath, don't you?" Fighting off a string of wet canine kisses, she dragged the dog away to where a curious passerby shooed him away from the shops. He wasn't a bad dog, just a little unruly. If only Miss Fairchild hadn't made such a fuss, she wouldn't have gotten the pup so riled up.

"Th-th-thank you, Drake."

Charlotte let out a deep breath. "Haven't you ever had a dog?"

"Of course not! Why anyone would intentionally keep such a beast is beyond me."

The momentary guilt Charlotte was feeling disappeared as quickly as it came. Because Charlotte loved dogs—more so, even than a few human's she knew.

"You're all right now. He didn't hurt you, did he?" Charlotte patted the taller girl's arm.

"I don't like dogs!" Her mistress wailed. "You took too long in the shop. You should have returned in a more timely fashion."

"I'm sorry, Sus– Miss." Charlotte *had* spent additional time selecting gifts for Lord Mapleton's mother and sister. She'd not deny she'd taken advantage of the situation.

And she'd chosen a ghastly perfume for Miss Fairchild's gift.

Quickly locating a handkerchief from a pocket, Charlotte dabbed at Susan's reddened cheeks and then a few smudges on her sleeve. "I merely wished to be certain your gift was perfect and took rather longer than I ought. Please forgive me."

She did feel badly. Miss Fairchild might actually like dogs if her parents had allowed her a pet as a child. "He wasn't going to hurt you, but how could you have known?" Except for the wagging of his tail and the giant smile on his face.

Because contrary to what some people thought, dogs most definitely smiled.

"I didn't know. But he kept jumping on me. He wouldn't leave me alone." A calm began settling on the frightened young woman.

"He wanted your pie." Charlotte held back a chuckle.

"I'd have gladly given it to him, if I'd known." Susan sniffed. "Thank you." She added. "For saving me."

Relief swept through Charlotte--relief that her mistress was not truly harmed and also that since she'd 'saved' Miss Fairchild, she apparently hadn't placed her job in jeopardy again.

She needed this position. Oliver would slay her if she turned up unemployed for a fourth time.

"Miss Fairchild!"

Having exited Mr. Blanchard's shop, Lord Mapleton took one look at Susan's distraught expression and sprinted across the road. "What happened? Damn my eyes but I shouldn't have left you unattended. My abject apologies, Miss Fairchild." He was glancing around as though looking for a thief or murderer. And then his gaze settled on Susan's dress, where streaks of mud soiled the skirt. The Earl furrowed his brows. "Who did this?"

"It was a dog, my lord." Charlotte did not look at him while she spoke, thinking that he might feel as guilty as she did. "She is afraid of them."

"He was huge! A veritable monster! Giant teeth and the very devil's eyes! He all but attacked me in the street." Susan's tears started up all over again as she crumpled into Lord Mapleton's arms. "I hate dogs!"

"There, there. He didn't bite you, did he?" The Earl stroked Susan's back and glancing up, finally caught Charlotte's gaze with a sheepish look. Ah, yes. She'd had the right of it.

She saw something else in his eyes, though. If Charlotte were to hazard a guess, she'd wager that Lord Mapleton kept a dog for a pet. Or perhaps two. Such a gentleman as him likely loved animals.

Not an auspicious indication of the couple's future wedded bliss.

"He wanted her meat pie." Charlotte flicked her eyes to the ground at the crushed pastry which hadn't survived the attack after all. Hopefully the mutt would return and find it before it was no more than crumbs in the dirt. "He was quite exuberant about it." She shrugged.

"Drake took forever to return." Miss Fairchild complained. But then she noticed the package Lord Mapleton clutched beneath his arm. "Oh, my present! What is it? Are you going to give it to me today?"

The size of the package lent Charlotte to believe that he'd purchased all of her recommended items. He'd valued her suggestions for his sister and mother, she'd been certain. But did he now regret his approval of the dreadful perfume?

And what about after he'd married Miss Fairchild? He would know Charlotte hadn't exhibited loyalty for her employer. Charlotte cringed inside. Judging by Susan and the Viscountess' outlook, the betrothal was as good as done. Lord Mapleton could very well be her future employer.

She'd best prepare herself. Control her impulses. Curb her tongue.

Although she wondered at her ability to make such changes now, when she'd been unable to at any of her other posts...

Charlotte bit her lip.

If she hadn't been raised by a vicar, she could have contemplated other means for making a living. Many women who chose to be some gentleman's mistress were well provided for. If she thought she had any talent, she could have found it interesting to try being a dancing girl, or a seamstress in a theatre. She could have served ale in a tavern.

Perhaps.

She might have enjoyed almost anything more than the tedium of her current situation. She could not imagine disliking any of those other positions with quite so much passion.

Or performing them any worse.

ANTHONY CHASTISED himself all the way back to Viscount Denton's estate as the phaeton rumbled along.

He could not--he absolutely *would* not--allow an inconsequential woman, with eyes the color of the sea, to upend his plans.

He'd already contracted the foreman to commence with more rebuilding and land improvements. He had little time for courting. He'd considered participating in the great marriage mart in London this spring, but the fire had expedited his need. The season in London would not commence for several months.

Jilting his neighbor's daughter was not an option.

He'd suggested this outing in order to get to know *Miss Drake* better.

He blinked.

Miss Fairchild--not *Miss Drake*!

All he'd discovered thuslywas that Miss Fairchild hated dogs. Surely, she would feel differently upon meeting Rufus and Walter. Anthony had had both dogs for nearly nine years now. Before that, he'd had Fritz for nearly fourteen.

He could not remember a time in his life when he'd not enjoyed the companionship of his own, or one of his father's hounds.

He swallowed hard and turned his thoughts back to his present surroundings.

"Are you warm enough?" he lowered his mouth so that she would be sure to hear him. "Susan?" He'd not addressed her yet by her given name. But he had to make progress in his suit today. Up until yesterday, he'd considered himself reasonably attracted to Miss Drake.

Miss Fairchild. He'd considered himself reasonably attracted to *Miss Fairchild.*

Although the sun just barely peeked through a thin layer of clouds, the breeze carried a chill. The lady beside him apparently noticed his intimate gesture but rather than show any pleasure, tightened her lips. "I am well enough, my lord."

It seemed she'd not yet forgiven him for withholding her gift until Christmas day, when it would be more appropriate. She'd begged and cajoled incessantly, like a spoiled child, but he'd stood his ground. To present her with a gift too early would cause scandal.

He'd wait until she was his fiancé.

The thought cooled him more than the wind.

Only two days until Christmas.

Silence hovered the remainder of the drive, but for the creaking sounds of the turning wheels. As Glenstone Hollow drew near, Anthony contemplated speaking with her father this afternoon. He could make his official request for her hand and discuss contracts. He would then return the next morning to formally offer for the girl herself.

Damn, but his valet had knotted his cravat tightly today.

Again.

Two manservants approached the landau as the horses slowed to a halt in front of the elegant manor. The taller of them opened the door while the other lowered the step and assisted Miss Fairchild and then Miss Drake onto solid ground.

Anthony fought the urge to secretly grasp the maid's hand, as though she needed his reassurances –– as though he had any right whatsoever. What on earth was the matter with him?

Instead, he rose and then followed reluctantly. Miss Fairchild awaited him at the bottom of the steps leading inside.

He bowed.

"I will see you later tonight then?" Miss Fairchild reminded him.

He'd nearly forgotten about the invitation to dine with Lord Denton and his family and guests that evening.

"I'll be counting the minutes." Even he nearly winced at himself this time.

He would not speak with the viscount about marriage contracts today.

She lifted her chin in a jerking motion. "Indeed." And then addressing Miss Drake. "Fetch my parasol from Lord Mapleton's vehicle."

"Of course." Miss Drake backed away from both of them, looking as uncomfortable as he felt.

But beautiful, by God.

He shook his head in a futile attempt to dismiss such thoughts and bowed once again in the general direction of his prospective fiancé. "Good day, Miss Fairchild."

"Until this evening, Lord Mapleton." And with a pout,

she disappeared inside without affording him another glance.

He rather deserved it.

Because all thoughts of Susan Fairchild disappeared the moment she did.

Miss Drake had hopped a few times and seemed to be wiggling her behind as she struggled to climb back onto the landau. She'd almost succeeded only to fall backward, one foot remaining on the high step revealing a finely shaped ankle for him to ogle.

"Charlotte!" He stepped forward and took hold of her waist. Instead of assisting her up right away, however, he leaned forward and inhaled. "I'll retrieve it for you."

But neither moved. In fact, his hands grasped her tighter.

God, this was inappropriate. Dishonorable. Reprehensible even. He lashed a thousand other insults at himself but still refused to let her go.

He imagined his hands sliding around her waist--tugging her flush up against him so that he could cradle her softness with his body. He imagined removing her bonnet so that he could see if her hair was as golden as he'd imagined it to be. And then dropping his lips to taste the skin along her neck.

"My lord." The words emerged from her on a gasp. "Please."

Please what? Release her? Leave her be? Or spin her around and claim her lips with his own.

The sound of a male voice clearing nearby jolted him. One of the manservants.

Miss Drake practically flew into the vehicle, quickly

located the parasol and scrambled back out. Anthony made no attempt to assist her this time.

"Charlotte." He could not resist saying her name. Anything to delay her disappearance. She halted and then turned slowly to face him.

Her eyes reflected the same tumult he felt.

But she shook her head. "I--cannot. You..." She shook her head again, and then more firmly. "I am Drake."

Yes. She could not be Charlotte to him. And yet he stepped forward, eliminating all but a few feet of distance between them. "Miss Drake. Yes. But thank you. Both my mother and my sister will be happy with their gifts." Taking hold of her free hand, he lifted it to his lips and bowed.

Her fingers were slim and fragile, as he'd expected. Her subtle fragrance tantalized him, as he'd expected. His lips craved to touch more than just her gloves, as he damn well knew they would.

What he'd *not* expected was the wave of rightness that crashed over him in that moment. As though he'd found a missing part of himself.

But when he glanced back up her expression tore at his heart. Because again, he recognized all of his own longing reflected there, but along with that, he saw what he could only conclude to be fear.

No, not fear, he corrected himself. Sheer terror.

CHAPTER 5

IMPOSSIBLE THOUGHTS

Charlotte sighed heavily.

The trip into town had been nothing less than a disaster.

But wonderful.

Tragically wonderful.

Because her heart had cracked wide open. Yes, such a thought aptly described the pain inside her chest. And now her splintered heart was causing intermittent bursts of elation, quickly followed by equally powerful catapults into devastation.

Foolishness! She knew better. To give into such an attraction meant only one thing for a servant girl. Her father would roll over in his grave if she were to go that route. He'd roll over if he knew she'd contemplated it even for a second.

Which she had not.

Pressing and brushing clothing allowed her far too much time to mull over the hopelessness of all of it. Perhaps she'd been mistaken. She'd imagined the earl's attentions.

She hadn't eaten anything that morning. Would not that cause her to feel so lightheaded in his company?

But when Miss Fairchild began talking of her pending betrothal, a heavy sadness invaded her soul.

"He ought to have given me the gift, wouldn't you agree? I hadn't thought that he might be so stuffy, but he is considerably older… So very rude of him, though. For as long as I can remember, Lord Mapleton has been my father's choice, but not mine. His lordship can be awfully dull, you know. And he's not as good looking as his brother." Miss Fairchild examined herself in the looking glass and sighed. "Lord Mapleton is the earl, though. He holds the title. How could I settle for anything less?"

"How indeed?" Charlotte mumbled. She'd brought out a red velvet evening gown for Miss Fairchild to wear to dinner and spread it across the bed.

Charlotte's father, as a well-liked vicar, had introduced Charlotte to more than a few prospective husbands over the years. Tall ones, short ones, fat ones, thin ones, a few had even been handsome and one of the older ones had been wealthy. In each of them, she'd looked for that special elusive *something*, that feeling, of wanting and of needing. That feeling that *this was the one*.

But she'd not once come even close to finding it. So impractical! And the interest had dwindled to a trickle. Her last proposal was 3 years ago. Gentlemen weren't interested in marrying vicar's daughters who had achieved such and age as she had: six and twenty. In four years she would be thirty!

"His estate is grander than Papa's." Miss Fairchild added. "I'll never want for anything."

Charlotte tidied the lovely rose down with a soft brush.

Miss Fairchild would look pretty in this color, rather than the pastels she normally wore. Her own brown skirt resembled a rag in comparison.

Perhaps Charlotte ought to have been more like Susan. Perhaps she ought to have exhibited such practicality. If she'd done that, she wouldn't be working as a servant today.

Tears pricked the back of Charlotte's eyes at the thought of lost opportunities, but she blinked them away, angry with herself for such futile thoughts.

When Lord Mapleton's lips had touched her hand, she'd thought for an instant that all was right with her world. She'd ceased to be one person, alone, fighting for a place to belong. No, she had found her match, her other half.

But in the same instant, horror had fallen on her like a mountain of rock.

He was not for her.

He was an earl. He was also a day or two away from being betrothed to her mistress.

"I won't require your attendance at dinner this evening. Mother says you'd make the numbers uneven." Susan's voice changed from a confidante to a superior. "Wait up for me regardless. I realize all of this…" she fluttered her hands in the air, "is new to you. But I don't see why I should be prevailed up to suffer for your inadequacies."

Charlotte was not a fool. She was well aware that her duties were not fulfilled until her mistress was abed. But instead of saying as much, she nodded. Another facet of servant life that would drain the very life from her soul.

She hadn't minded hauling buckets of steaming water that morning, sewing until her eyes ached nor performing other menial tasks.

It was the lack of respect. The lack of dignity afforded

most servants… Her soul fought and then died a little each time one of her employers referred to themselves as her 'better.'

"I'll be waiting right here, Miss Fairchild." Charlotte forced a lilt to her voice. She would have preferred to grumble. How hard could it be to wait up a few hours so she could help Susan prepare for bed?

Several hours later Charlotte rubbed sleep from her eyes. She stretched in an attempt to rouse herself from the loveseat in Miss Fairchild's suite. When she'd searched the room earlier for something to read, so she could stay awake, she'd only located a few fashion magazines and unfinished letters. She'd only meant to close her eyes for a few minutes.

She was not the world's best companion, but she would succeed. She must.

Tired but restless, Charlotte rose and drifted toward the window. She could slip into the garden for just a moment. She touched the window. The air outside would be cold.

She'd only take a few seconds for herself. And then when she returned, she'd be more wakeful and ready to assist Miss Fairchild into her bed.

Since Charlotte's own bedchamber consisted of a small cot in the dressing room, she didn't have to go far to locate her coat and hat. And a scarf that her father had told her once belonged to her mother.

She slipped into the corridor and then tiptoed down the main staircase. Murmurs of conversation drifted up from the drawing rooms followed by occasional bursts of laughter. Who was she in this world? Did she belong anywhere anymore?

Outside alone, she could almost imagine she was her father's daughter again. An icy breeze rustled a few remaining leaves in the trees, the moon shone like a beacon. For a few precious minutes, she could imagine herself a normal young woman with normal wants, normal tasks, and normal expectations.

A normal life.

Contentment teased her as she strode along the dirt path. Ten minutes, she'd only take these ten minutes to herself. She could pretend…

"You may kiss me if you wish." Susan's voice drifted through the trees, halting Charlotte in her tracks. She should have known others might be outside. With a house full of guests for the pending holiday at least a few of them would wish to seek privacy in the nearly dormant but still lovely, garden.

Her breath caught as she listened for Lord Mapleton's response. Of course, her mistress would be with Lord Mapleton. Who else would she give permission to kiss her?

But there was no response. Only silence.

That meant…

Apparently intent upon torturing herself, Charlotte pinched her eyes together as she imagined the handsome earl taking Miss Fairchild into his arms, his mouth claiming the other woman's lips.

She swallowed around the suddenly large lump that had formed in her throat. Did this mean the two of them had finally become engaged?

"Shall we return to the others then? They'll be missing us." Yes, it was Lord Mapleton's voice.

"Already? We just came outside."

A growl? Or was Lord Mapleton clearing his throat? He didn't sound as though he was overcome with passion for his fiancé. "I do not wish to offend your father."

Feminine laughter. "Papa won't mind. In fact, I think he rather expects–"

"I will not dishonor you, Miss Fairchild." An edge in his voice this time, as though the lady had irritated him.

Charlotte could picture her mistress' pout. Miss Fairchild was accustomed to getting everything she wanted.

"Will you be meeting with him tomorrow then? Christmas is the day after. Everyone expects an announcement at the ball."

More clearing of the throat, an almost gurgling sound this time, as though he was choking.

"It is something that you wish, then?" If Charlotte was not mistaken, this was as good as a proposal, was it not?

"Yes, oh, yes, my lord! You will speak with Father then?"

Charlotte's heart shattered into a million pieces and her knees nearly buckled beneath her. It was better this way. Better to not create any fantasies about a man she could never have. She'd been foolish to get caught up in his smoldering stares and kind smile.

"I will."

And then more silence. Charlotte pinched her eyes together again.

"Come, Miss Fairchild, I'll return you inside now." His voice strained, almost as though he was experiencing breathing difficulties.

Charlotte waited until she knew they were gone and then dropped onto a nearby bench.

Miss Fairchild might be retiring to her chamber anytime now. Charlotte needed to return inside but her legs refused to obey. She was trapped. Trapped in her person. Trapped by circumstance. Trapped by fate.

How long she sat there, she couldn't say. She only knew

that she hated this new person she'd been forced to become. She should have married one of the gentlemen her father had chosen for her.

Lord Mapleton and Miss Fairchild were affianced to one another. It was no longer merely a possibility. Charlotte had heard it with her own ears.

And he'd kissed his betrothed. Perhaps twice.

"What are you doing out here? It's not safe for a lady to sit along in the dark, you know."

MISS DRAKE BURST off the bench at his words. He reached out to steady her when she seemed to sway.

"I must go inside. Miss Fairchild will be needing me."

If he'd not been grasping her arm, he was certain she would have bolted.

She'd taken his breath away when he first caught sight of her sitting alone. Without the ridiculous cap, she'd unwittingly revealed herself to be even more of a beauty.

Not a golden blond, but the color of white sand. It might be a trick of the moonlight, but he did not think so.

"Miss Fairchild seems quite content to remain downstairs for a while longer." He reassured the woman who'd managed to take over most of his thoughts.

Miss Fairchild had entered the drawing room and immediately joined a few of her cousins for a rousing game of charades. Anthony had excused himself, informing her that he'd forgotten his cane outside. In truth, he hadn't brought a cane with him tonight, let alone out into the garden. *His fiancé* had merely smiled agreeably and turned to hear something fascinating that Mr. Creighton was saying.

Anthony's throat constricted at the thought that she'd tell any of them of his 'proposal.' And of her acceptance.

Dear God.

Asking her had not been his intention at all. One moment he'd been testing the waters and the next a noose had dropped around his neck.

He released Charlotte's arm. *Miss Drake's* arm. He had no right to think of her by her Christian name, let alone touch her with such familiarity. And yet she'd not chastised him for it. And she had not bolted inside as he'd feared she might.

But then the realization of her location struck him. "You have been outside for long?" Had she overheard what had become his proposal?

She nodded, her eyes answering the question he'd not uttered aloud.

"Congratulations are in order, then?" She smiled weakly.

This was not what he wanted!

What could he say to this lady? Since first setting eyes upon her he'd wanted something… He'd felt as though he'd known her forever, and yet he yearned to begin to learn everything about her.

"Are you… growling?"

Anthony glanced up at the odd question. But, *oh, hell.* Daphne had accused him of growling for as long as he could remember.

But Miss Drake was laughing. It was a joyous sound that rivalled sleigh bells.

"You were!" she accused. "You were growling! I asked

you if congratulations were in order and you growled at me! Like a giant boar!"

How could he not join in her amusement? Drawing one hand through his hair, he smiled sheepishly into those lovely eyes of hers. "And what if I was?"

"Growling generally does not convey pleasure." She sobered.

At the reminder of what had occurred not thirty minutes earlier, another growl escaped—this one noticeable even to himself. "I did not intend to ask her in that moment. The question was hypothetical. I was asking her if... *If* I were to ask. I was not asking the question itself, per se." He moaned and then dropped onto the bench Charlotte had just vacated.

"You kissed her." Her voice was near. He didn't need to look up to know that she'd lowered herself to sit beside him. He could feel her presence. She exerted an attraction unlike any he'd known.

He'd hoped that kissing Miss Fairchild would ignite something similar inside of him. It had done the opposite. "I had thought perhaps..." Anthony glanced sideways and forgot what he'd been going to say.

Why this woman? Charlotte Drake was a servant for God's sake! Frustration turned to outright anger. By no means had he chosen Miss Fairchild lightly. He'd found himself backed into a corner by circumstances beyond his control. Not for a million years would he marry in such a calculated manner if conditions did not demand it. He would not be the person to suffer if the betrothal fell through. That would fall to others–to tenants and workers. Tenant families.

"Do you know how many families lost their homes in

that infernal fire? How many merchants lost their shops in addition to their inventories? I've poured every penny I can into rebuilding that village. Can you begin to understand that? It's not as though I have a choice..." His voice sounded gruffer than normal. It didn't make sense that he should express himself thusly with Charlotte. She deserved none of this, and yet he was working himself into a most resentful state. How dare Miss Charlotte Drake come along with her sparkling intelligent eyes and full lips and delightful figure *now*? How dare fate set her in his path?

"Last summer I invested heavily in the canal system in the surrounding shire. Did you know that? Had I known the entire damn village would burn down I would not have spent so liberally. Families who've lived and worked on my family's estate for generations have roofs that leak every time it rains. Roofs I'd intended to have replaced before spring. Have you notice that there seems to be an abundance of rain in this wretched country of ours? And the foundation at Maplehurst is in need of repairs. I'll bet you didn't realize that, did you?"

He leaned into her. This close, the green specks in her eyes could almost be counted. "Do you know how much all of that costs? Money I don't have to spare right now."

She simply stared back at him, and then made a barely imperceptible shake of her head.

Feeling desperate, Anthony grasped her hands in his. She needed to understand this about him. She needed to understand what drove him and why he'd come to the decision he had.

"I've a reputation to maintain! I've a younger sister and brother who rely upon me! And not only them, but two aunts and an ailing mother. And employees. Tenants. I represent security to them. Permanence. It is a part of the title. It is a part of who I am."

And yet he leaned forward. Her warm, clean scent tantalized his senses, so much so that he could hardly keep himself from tasting her.

As though an invisible string wound itself around both of them, they'd inched closer and closer. Soon only a whisper separated their lips. "And Parliament." She reminded him with a hoarse voice. "I am not uninformed, you know."

"I did not mean to imply that you were." He could taste her breath on his lips. "Damn you, Charlotte."

Where had his anger gone? His frustration that she was mucking up all his plans evaporated.

He couldn't allow it.

He couldn't allow himself.

With a jerk, Anthony pulled himself away. "So, you see…"

She stared at the hand of hers that he'd just released and then looked up to meet his eyes.

"I see all right. I've seen all along." She blinked once and tilted her head. "It is you who is being a slow top. Why are you sitting here talking to me? I certainly hope you aren't expecting... Because I will not. I am not."

He deserved it. He deserved her to slap him and then walk away, never to look back. But she did neither.

"And stop growling at me."

"I'm not growling at you." He huffed.

"You were."

"Grrrr." Perhaps he had been. "I know I shouldn't be sitting here talking with you. And yet... it's the only place I wish to be right now. Believe it or not, I'm making every possible effort to avoid you."

"Might I suggest you're failing miserably?"

Resting his elbows on his knees, he buried his head in both hands. "As I'm mucking this up, perhaps you'd do well to stay away from me in the future." It was the last thing he wanted, and yet the only thing that made sense.

"That's the trouble, my lord," A heavy sigh fell between them. "I haven't the option. You forget that my livelihood depends upon my ability to keep Miss Fairchild happy. I have no choice but to be at the beck and call of the woman who is your fiancé, now. I haven't the choice of taking off for a brief holiday in London." She tried to sound flippant, but he heard something in her voice that hadn't been there before.

Hopelessness?

"I have trouble thinking of you as a servant." God but he'd made a mess of everything. The truth of the matter was, she didn't seem like any servant he'd ever known. "You don't look like a servant, or act like a servant. Something in your eyes perhaps. Intelligence, damnit. And pride!"

"Would you like to watch me empty a few chamber pots? Or perhaps have a look at the cot I sleep on now?" She ought to hate him.

Good lord, this was not her fault. "I deserve to be flayed. I know. And then crushed to pieces like those infernal dried up lapis of yours."

The trouble was that *he liked her*. He more than liked her, he experienced all the idiotic nonsense one reads about in poetry whenever she was near. He became tongue-tied, lost to only her.

"You are no wilting flower, my lord. More of an oak that

needs chopping down. But she'd turned to stare into his eyes and didn't look as though she wished to take an axe to him.

Because there was something between them. He could almost touch it, taste it… She knew it. He knew it.

Damn my eyes!

None of it mattered.

"I'll do better to keep a reasonable distance in the future." He practically choked on the promise. A few days ago, he could not have imagined feeling this way for anyone. But now… His heart skipped a beat to consider a world without her in it. And yet, he must.

"As will I."

Both sat unmoving until with a sigh, Charlotte rose from the bench. "Good night, my lord."

"Good night," but couldn't help himself. "Charlotte." Her name on his lips was as close as he'd get to ever touching her again.

It could not be goodbye, however. It might be easier if it could be. No, he would return tomorrow morning to go over contracts with Viscount Denton.

WEATHER TAKES A TURN

$\mathcal{A}$nthony awoke early, despite not leaving Lord Denton's estate until well past midnight. He'd avoided spirits last night but might as well have been soused for the blasted headache torturing him today.

"Not so tight, Penrose." Knowing Anthony was to make his official address to Lord Denton today, his fastidious valet had retied the blasted knot on his cravat seven times already. His hessians were buffed to a high shine and the coat and cravat pin draped nearby were the finest he owned.

When Anthony entered the breakfast room, he fought the urge to run back upstairs and change into his oldest riding clothes. Anything to avoid this meeting today.

Daphne glanced up from where she sat nibbling on a piece of toast and raised her brows. Michael turned a page of the newspaper he was reading.

"You're going then?" Daphne would know the status of his plans.

Michael lowered the paper and flicked his gaze toward

the window. No sunlight this morning. In fact, a few almost imperceptible snowflakes drifted from the sky. "Bad weather, old chap. Send your excuses and remain at home. We'll finish off that bottle of scotch over cards."

"She is expecting you?" His sister held rather more reverence for the ways of the world.

"Worse than that." Anthony grabbed a small plate and collected eggs and sausage from the layout on the sideboard. "Her father is."

"Oh, dear." She sipped her coffee and grimaced. Glancing toward the window herself, she then added, "I don't suppose a few snowflakes are reason enough to cry off. Take plenty of lap blankets and a brick for your feet."

Whereas Michael approached life recklessly, Daphne was the worrier. She worried about their mother. She worried about various tenants. She worried about Michael and, most of all, she worried about her oldest brother.

Although a brisk ride through the frigid air seemed just what he needed, he couldn't trust himself not to keep riding right on past Glenstone Hollow and onward to London.

And beyond.

"I'll order a warm brick." He reassured her.

After all was settled, this coming spring he would take Daphne into London for her own coming out. His wife could sponsor her. Her dowry could pay for it.

Their mother had already confined herself to her chamber when Daphne became of age. As her older brother, he experienced reluctance at setting her loose amongst London's elite. He'd told her more than once that he'd be content to keep her home and she'd not argued with him. But it wouldn't be fair to her. She deserved the opportunity to find her own place in life.

Daphne was something of a beauty. Anthony, being one of the male species himself, knew better than to trust half the gentlemen of the ton. He would vet his sister's prospective suitors carefully. He'd be damned if anyone would take advantage of her under his watch.

She would have all of his protection.

But that Charlotte Drake had the same. He'd never considered himself someone who would pray upon an innocent servant. The bite of eggs he'd swallowed practically curdled in his stomach.

"Mama seemed better this morning." Daphne interrupted his thoughts. "She ate most of her breakfast and then refused to move from the window. I think she remembers the snow. Do you think she knows it's almost Christmas?"

He'd wondered the same last year. And the one before that.

"She loved Christmas." An image flitted through his memory of a younger version of their mother and father celebrating the winter holidays long ago. He'd hoped to recreate similar events for his own family one day. "I purchased her gift yesterday." And in a million years he couldn't have found a more perfect one.

He vaguely wondered if Charlotte liked being outdoors when it snowed. Had her parents played with her as a child? Did she have any siblings?

He'd dreamt of her last night. She'd been his wife and they had two children. A boy and a girl. And then she'd been in his bed, beneath him.

With a screech of his chair, he erupted from the table. "No reason to delay any longer."

Daphne rose more slowly. "Be careful. If the weather worsens, don't attempt to return today."

But today was Christmas Eve. He'd not abandon his family on Christmas. Betrothal or not.

He kissed his sister on the cheek lightly, appreciating her steady support.

Rather than order the carriage he strolled outside to the stable himself. He'd find it too difficult to sit still for the twenty minutes the stable hands required to complete the task. The job would be over quicker with his assistance and he'd not be given so much time to think.

The decision was out of his hands now.

The matter was settled.

He need only officially ask the viscount and sign the contracts.

Impatience to have it over with, along with an intense desire to delay the entire business, plagued him.

Despite the blowing snow and brisk wind, the drive to his neighbor's estate was over far too quickly. Knowing a sense of impending doom, Anthony gathered his hat and cane. Almost before the carriage drew to a halt, he threw open the door himself. He could not change his mind. He would not. It was impossible. In a resolute burst, he jumped to the ground and followed a footman inside the increasingly familiar foyer.

When the large maple doors closed shut behind him, beads of sweat trickled down the back of his neck. It would soon be over. It would be done.

"If you'll follow me, my lord," Mr. Tresham, the well-dressed butler smiled tightly. "I'll see if Lord Denton can meet with you."

So, Anthony was the one to be kept waiting now. He glanced around the elegantly furnished drawing room where most of the entertaining had taken place last night and tugged at his cravat. A fire burned in the hearth and was emitting an uncomfortable amount of heat. He paced across the room a few times before taking a seat in one of the hardback chairs.

What was Miss Drake doing this morning? He swallowed hard, disgusted with himself for failing to keep in mind their vastly different stations.

She'd have risen hours ago. Were her tasks limited to taking care of Miss Fairchild? Or did the housekeeper demand more of her?

Anthony clenched his jaw. He hated the thought of her toiling on hands and knees, or trudging up and down the stairs with buckets of water. Was she required to assist with the laundry? He remembered how dried and irritated the laundry woman's hands had been the last time he'd paid any attention.

Which had been years ago.

He hadn't taken much notice of most servants. But for the cook, the housekeeper and his valet.

He erupted out of the seat, unable to remain still, and crossed to the window. What had been tiny flurries of snow had turned to giant flakes swirling angrily. Hell and damnation, he needed to get this over with and be on his way.

He wasn't sure if he felt relief or nausea at the reappearance of Mr. Tresham.

"His Lordship has yet to rise. Lady Denton and Miss Fairchild shall be down shortly, however."

Blast it all. Anthony nodded. Lord Denton had consumed an abundance of port the evening before and probably needed to sleep it off.

The windowpanes rattled and Anthony grimaced. If this weather didn't let up, he wasn't going anywhere soon. It wouldn't be fair of him to put his cattle and driver in danger merely because he preferred to be somewhere else. Anywhere but here.

He should have waited until tomorrow. Christmas Day.

"My Lord, how wonderful to see you this morning." Lady Denton appeared, elegantly dressed. Miss Fairchild entered close behind. "I'm so sorry his lordship is indisposed." She winced. "But perhaps you can meet with him later this afternoon. I can't imagine you're going anywhere in this awful storm."

"My lord." Miss Fairchild dropped into a curtsy beside her mother. She seemed paler than usual this morning, as though she'd lain awake much of the night as he had.

Anthony bowed. "Miss Fairchild."

"Tresham." Lady Denton beckoned out the door to the butler. "Fetch Drake so that Lord Mapleton and Miss Fairchild can be properly chaperoned. I promised Mrs. Smythe I'd show her the gallery this morning."

"Of course, my lady." The efficient butler removed himself as quickly as he'd appeared.

Drake. Miss Drake.

Charlotte.

Anthony ran one hand through his hair. Damn his eyes, but this was not going to get any easier.

CHARLOTTE GLANCED out the window from Miss Fairchild's chamber. He must be eager to settle the betrothal with her father to have traveled in this weather.

Miss Fairchild had been unusually quiet when she'd finally returned to her chamber late the night before. Charlotte had thought the younger girl would have been pleased with herself, but instead, she'd seemed subdued. In fact, she'd barely said a word while Charlotte prepared her for bed.

She'd actually thanked Charlotte when she'd finished plaiting her hair. And she hadn't mentioned Lord Mapleton even once.

As much as Charlotte had dreaded hearing Miss Fairchild rehash the proposal, she knew that being a confidante was, in fact, one of her duties. Why wasn't Susan reveling in the proposal?

Even this morning Lady Denton had ordered her daughter to dress carefully. For a moment Charlotte had thought Susan looked paler than usual at the reminder.

It was almost as though she was having second thoughts.

Which ought not to affect Charlotte at all. If Susan called it off, Lord Mapleton would merely need to find another gently bred and well dowered young woman.

Charlotte would not be required to hear about it if that were the case. She wouldn't have to fear that she would see him. She wouldn't have to pretend she'd never seen longing in his eyes. If he married some other lady, Charlotte could go about her work and forget he even existed. That would be far superior to living as a servant in his household.

So perhaps it made a difference after all.

A tremor ran through her as she smoothed the soft moss day gown she'd chosen for her young mistress. The color softened Susan's features without overpowering her coloring. The coiffure Charlotte created turned out rather delightful, what with all the delicate braids and a few curls.

No matter that she'd had to redo the style three times before getting it right.

Susan had looked lovely when her mother demanded she accompany her downstairs.

Tidying the suddenly quiet chamber, Charlotte scooped up Susan's night dress and draped the fine material over the back of a chair.

A knock interrupted her musings.

"Miss Drake," Mr. Tresham peered in. "Her ladyship requests you come downstairs to chaperone Miss Fairchild right away. His Lordship, Lord Mapleton, that is, will be staying for the day."

How was it possible that her heart took flight and yet plummeted at the exact same time?

"They are in the East Drawing room." And with a nod he disappeared.

Charlotte caught sight of herself in the mirror. Dark circles etched below her eyes. Taking a moment, she wound her own braid atop her head and then donned the required mop cap all maids wore. She wished she had a prettier dress to wear than the brown muslin, but then scoffed at the thought. Even if she had been able to bring along some of her old wardrobe, she could not have worn them as a companion. Lady Denton had been perfectly clear about that on her first day there.

"You can do this." She whispered at her reflection. She was to act as chaperone. Very well. A good chaperone remained invisible and provided assistance to her mistress. Charlotte would tiptoe inside and keep her gaze on the floor.

She wouldn't look at him. She wouldn't even peek to see if he looked tired, or relieved, or if he was looking at her.

Charlotte would do her best to ignore the courting couple. She'd keep her mind on other matters.

If only she could bring a book with her.

She'd not dwell on the fact that this was the first Christmas she'd spend without her father. The Denton household, filled with guests for the holidays, required extra work from all the servants. Most of the servants grumbled that Christmas didn't allow for much celebration by the lower classes, but that they quite looked forward to Boxing Day.

She must do her best to do the same.

The storm swirling outside seemed almost magical though. Christmas was the season of hope. She'd do all she could to summon any measure of Christmas spirit that she could.

It's what her father would have wanted.

CHAPTER 7

SHARED INTERESTS

Charlotte wiggled uncomfortably in her chair. Since she'd tiptoed in and taken her seat in the formal drawing room, Lord Mapleton and Miss Fairchild had barely spoken ten words to one another. Which, if she was to guess, was more than they'd spoken before Charlotte had taken her unobtrusive seat near the door.

Oh, but this was excruciating.

Susan smoothed her gown. Lord Mapleton shifted in his seat.

The ticking of the clock on the mantle echoed loudly.

"Do you play chess, my lord?" The words sprung from Charlotte's lips before she could think. He glanced across the room at her with questioning eyes. He had done well to completely ignore her so far.

Which she'd appreciated.

On some levels. Her heart, of course, had not.

"Not with me, my lord," she clarified. Of course, he'd not think to play chess with her! "With Miss Fairchild. Do you play, Miss Fairchild?"

At this question, Susan scrunched her face up in distaste. "Heaven's no! Why would I waste my time learning to play a military game?"

"Oh, but chess is so much more--" Charlotte caught herself. She had spent hours across a board with her father on cold winter evenings, but this was not her place.

She dropped her gaze to her lap but felt Lord Mapleton's curious gaze, nonetheless.

Again, the ticking of the clock took prominence in the room. They all sat through two additional minutes of uncomfortable silence. She could not stand their discomfort. Anything was better than watching the two squirm and fidget. Charlotte wished she could be anywhere but here!

Hush Charlotte. Keep to yourself.

Lord Mapleton spoke. "Do you enjoy poetry, Miss Fairchild?"

"Doesn't everyone, my lord? Byron is simply all the rage!" Miss Fairchild fluttered a lacy fan below her chin.

Thank heavens!

Charlotte had read most of Lord Byron's works but by far preferred Keats. In her eyes, there was really no comparison. But at least these two might find something to converse upon.

"I met him once." The Earl grimaced. "The man certainly knows how to draw attention. What do you think of Wordsworth?"

Miss Fairchild frowned.

"Keats?" Her frown deepened.

"Wordsworth was one of my father's favorites." Charlotte piped up. She could not take a chance that this conversation would stall out again. "He refused to take Byron's poetry seriously, though. He considered his morality a threat to society. Did you know he kept a bear for a pet? Papa said the man walked him much as others walk their dogs."

"He does court controversy rather successfully." Lord Mapleton inserted. "One has to wonder if that isn't much of the reason for his success."

"And his politics are equally provoking. Art, poetry, even fashion can express ideas so much better than a political speech." Charlotte turned to Miss Fairchild, who'd seemed a trite lost at the conversation's turn. "Do you paint, Miss Fairchild? Or draw? I'm sure his lordship would be delighted to view your work..."

Grateful eyes flew open wide. Apparently, she'd felt as ill at ease as Charlotte -- perhaps more so. "Oh, yes. I don't show these to just anyone, my lord. They are normally for my eyes only." And then instead of asking Charlotte to fetch them, she burst from her seat. "Charlotte would never locate them as I keep them in a special hiding place. I shall return shortly."

Leaving Charlotte alone with Lord Mapleton.

Whereupon, an altogether different tension sprang up in the room. Charlotte forced her gaze to her hands. Was he looking at her? Was he as uncomfortable as she?

"Do you prefer Wordsworth?" His tentative question came as a surprise. He asked as though he was truly interested in her thoughts.

For three months now she'd gone without another human being asking her opinion on something other than themselves. Does this color suit me? Shall I wear the necklace or the broach? Do you think he'll send me flowers?

Nothing to do with herself. Nothing to make her feel as though she mattered in any way whatsoever.

Lord Mapleton had asked her opinion about a poet. He wanted to know *her thoughts* about a philosopher. Fighting the burning behind her eyes, she nodded and looked up to meet his gaze. "His works make me think about life, in general. Its purpose. Its meaning. But also, the little things and how precious they are..."

"Do you have a favorite?" Before he even finished asking, she was shaking her head.

"Never for long. Since my father died, one in particular comes to mind, *I've Wandered Lonely as a Cloud*." She sighed.

"But he is not lonely."

"No. He finds joy in a past experience." The poem offered hope that joy could be relived.

"So, you remember times with your father." Lord Mapleton's eyes reflected understanding. "And you are attempting to find joy now, in your memories."

Surely joy could not only be a thing of the past. Surely, she would know joy again. The alternative was unthinkable...

"Yes." She answered truthfully. Why would she tell him something so personal? Already, he must pity her for the station she held. She jutted her chin up, unwilling to accept his pity. "Did you imagine I couldn't read?"

His eyes held no pity, though. Just a sad understanding.

Why him? And why now?

"Never." And then she could see his throat work, as though swallowing some unwanted emotion.

What was taking Susan so long?

"Wordsworth is not my favorite though. Nor is Lord Byron. I prefer Keats, in case you wondered."

He laughed. Over the next several moments the two of them argued back and forth the merits of all three. Then she mentioned Jane Austin, an author Charlotte had discovered the year before.

Lord Mapleton was just promising he'd read one of Austin's works when Lady Denton appeared. She immediately sent a smile in Lord Mapleton's direction. But when she glanced around the room she frowned when her gaze landed on Charlotte and not her daughter.

"Miss Fairchild wanted to fetch some of her artwork." Lord Mapleton drew the perturbed woman's attention back toward himself. "And she insisted Charlotte would never be able to locate them."

"*Charlotte?*" Her ladyship's brows rose as she drew out Miss Drake's Christian name. "Drake." Her voice sounded icily cold as she addressed Charlotte now. "You'll attend to my daughter. She likely is in need of your assistance."

"Of course." Charlotte rose and dropped into a hurried curtsy before leaving the room.

What had she done now?

Lady Denton, Anthony belatedly realized, was all too aware that the companion attending her daughter was far more attractive than her daughter herself. He wondered how she'd allowed Charlotte to be hired in the first place. She'd likely told the vicar she'd hire the girl before seeing her in person. In his experience, ladies didn't favor having their servants outshine their offspring.

And damn his eyes, he'd referred to her as *Charlotte*.

Miss Fairchild and Charlotte rejoined them a few

minutes later. He was not surprised when Lady Denton immediately sent Charlotte away.

Again, he'd put her position in jeopardy.

Doing his best to redirect the Viscountess' suspicions, he made the proper comments and sounds of appreciation as Miss Fairchild explained her drawings. Even as he did this, he thoughts were never far from Charlotte.

"And this is a new style of dress I've designed that a lady can wear in the afternoons." He focused his eyes on the portrayal of a woman with sleeves the size of watermelons and nodded vaguely.

"Lovely." He murmured noncommittally.

The few moments he'd spent talking with Charlotte had been the most pleasant in recent memory. Her eyes had sparkled as she'd argued how romance involved politics. And by god, she'd had a point. Was it possible that he might be as attracted to her intelligence as he was to her countenance?

Or did his emotions go beyond that? Was it possible that two people were created for one another at the onset of their existence? The woman had quite thrown him for a loop. He'd never believed in such folly.

To be honest with himself, he'd never believed in love—the romantic kind, that was. He believed in familial love, which developed over years, cultivated with loyalty and responsibility.

"Would you care to take a stroll to the orangery?" Miss Fairchild touched his arm.

He'd barely been aware that she had set her artwork aside.

He glanced out to see the storm had increased in its

intensity. Damned if he wasn't trapped here for the day, and likely the night. He scrubbed one hand down his face.

Anything would be better than spending his time looking at fashion drawings. "I'd be delighted."

And so, he spent the next hour strolling through Viscount Denton's manor, all the while, enduring conversation as stilted as it had been before Charlotte joined them earlier.

In truth, worse.

When the sound of male laughter echoed into the foyer from the direction of the billiards room, Anthony sensed a chance for escape.

"Your cousins?" He flicked a glance in the direction the voices were coming from.

"And uncles. Do you play billiards, my lord? Do you enjoy it?" If he was not mistaken, she wished to escape him as well.

"Indeed." And then a hesitant step away from her. "Do you mind?"

A sound that resembled something in-between a choke and a laugh gurgled from her. He was right. Any attempt she made to hide her own relief right now would be quite futile. "I'm certain Mama has had a chamber prepared for you. Simply ask any of the servants when you're ready to retire." She walked backwards as she spoke.

And she was to be his wife.

No small amount of relief swept through him when he stepped into the all-male domain, decorated in rich heavy wooden tones. He was greeted heartily.

And scotch? Ah, yes. He'd love one.

And another. Ah yes, why not another?

Three hours later, he'd completely forgotten the reason

he'd come. Something to do with a marriage contract? He struggled to maintain his balance when finally going in search of a servant to show him to his room.

Not just any servant.

Charlotte.

CHAPTER 8

MUSIC OF THE HEART

Miraculously left alone for the afternoon, Charlotte searched out some lemon oil and a soft cloth. Ever since spying the gleaming piano in the seldom used music room, her first day as a member of the staff, she'd felt compelled to… polish it.

And it did, in fact, require dusting. Such a shame to ignore such a beautiful instrument for days on end. She sat down at the pianoforte and discovered her task for the afternoon.

The ivory keys were a dull, yellowish color. Taking a moment to fetch milk and a cleaning paste, time ceased to exist when she returned and set herself to scrubbing at each key individually. Occasionally, she'd set the cloth aside and allow her fingers to dance across them in one of her favorite runs. So caught up in the task was she that she didn't hear the door open. She only knew she was no longer alone, until an achingly familiar voice startled her.

"Charlotte."

She hadn't known him for even a week. Yet, in some ironic twist of fate, he'd come to mean the world to her.

Her fingers stilled. She glanced over her shoulder, and she let out a sigh of relief to discover that at least he'd come alone.

"My lord," she answered. Did he have need of her? Was he searching for her on Susan's request? Charlotte reluctantly pushed back the bench and began to rise.

"Don't get up on my behalf." He closed the door behind him and sauntered across the room. "You play?" Now he was standing, leaning really, against the wood she'd polished earlier.

Feeling self-conscious, she nodded. He should not be here. "I played for my father's congregation."

"You enjoy it." She glanced up briefly. His eyes were hooded and lazy. More sensual than normal…

"I do." She answered tentative. "Are you… well?"

He laughed, a low, ironic sounding chuckle. "As well as can be expected." And then, "Play for me?"

It could not hurt. Could it? Playing for others always gave her more pleasure than simply playing for herself. It forced her to concentrate harder. She tried to channel her emotions so the listener might feel the music as it was meant to be…

"Play something soothing."

It was Christmas, after all. She did not require sheet music for the song she had in mind. Immediately, she lost herself in her favorite carol. And she sang.

THE FIRST NOEL, *the Angel did say*
   Was to three poor Shepherds in fields as they lay.

In fields where they lay keeping their sheep,
In a cold winter's night that was so deep.
Noel, noel, noel, noel.
Born is the King of Israel.

SHE KNEW every verse by heart and finally finished up with
the last one.

IF WE IN our time shall do well
  We shall be free from death and Hell
  For God hath prepared for us all
  A resting place in general.

CHARLOTTE ENDED the final note tenderly. She had nearly
forgotten she wasn't alone. The song brought back so many
memories of her father, the life she knew…

"You've a gift." Lord Mapleton spoke the words softly.
"Both the playing and the singing."

Heat crawled up Charlotte's neck into her cheeks. She
wasn't embarrassed, but it had been so long since she'd been
paid a compliment. She blinked away a sudden stinging
behind her eyes. Music had always affected her emotionally.

"Thank you." She'd change the subject away from herself.
"Do you play?"

In answer, he walked closer and indicated she allow him
to join her on the bench. "Not as well as you. My mother
insisted we all take lessons at a young age."

He played some of the melody from another lively
Christmas carol. She joined him in adding to the song. At

the song's finish, they absorbed the silent peace that always followed music.

His touch had affected her before, almost beyond reason. But in that moment, without warning, the effect of his nearness was nearly too much to bear. His physical person tugged at her, like a magnet. To keep from leaning into him, she slid off her side of the bench. She retrieved the cloth she'd used earlier and wiped at the wooden cover.

"Originally this lovely instrument was called the *gravicembalo col piano e forte*." She needed to fill the silence between them before she said something she oughtn't. "It translates to 'keyboard instrument that's soft and loud.' Which is far too wordy and so it was shortened to pianoforte." She knew she was rambling. Likely she sounded like a stuffy governess––telling him something he already knew.

"Far too wordy." He watched her with a strange look in his eyes.

"Of course, the harpsichord came first. But it could not be played loudly or softly. It only had one volume. The instrument's limitations made it inferior to other instruments––music often expresses emotion through volume. In 1709, an Italian harpsichord maker named Bartolomeo di Francesco Cristofori created the *gravicembalo col piano e forte*. But you likely know that already..." Oh, lord, she'd practically been lecturing him.

"You're the damndest servant I've ever met." A half smile danced on his lips though.

"Your cravat's becoming untied."

A full smile now. "It's been choking me all week." He seemed far less brooding than he had when he initially entered the room.

"I'm sorry." Charlotte wasn't sure why she'd apologized. But yes, she was sorry that he had betrothed himself, sorry Miss Fairchild didn't understand the man he was.

"Why are you here?" He surprised her with such a question.

"You mean, here, in the music room? Or here working for Viscount Denton?"

"Your father passed away. Haven't you any family who could take you in?"

Oh… "I have a brother who lives on the outskirts of Bath. But he already has too many mouths to feed. And it isn't as though I'm not able bodied." She hated that this gentleman would feel pity for her. "It isn't as bad as it seems…" Only it was. She hated being a servant.

"Were you close to your father?"

Charlotte nodded. She pretended to have found a particular difficult smudge on the shining wood. Her father had been everything to her, even before Oliver had moved away. "His death came as a shock. Apoplexy. He'd always exhibited good health."

"I think you're likely to rub the shine right off of that." Charlotte didn't realize what he meant for a moment. Then she glanced up to see the teasing in his gaze. He had realized she was trying to avoid looking at him.

"I ought to see if Miss Fairchild has need of me." But he'd turned so that he was straddling the bench now, and caught at her wrist, preventing her escape.

"Let me enjoy you for these few minutes." He seemed far too serious. "Please," he added.

Charlotte swallowed hard. She wanted the same, but she had far more to lose than he.

"Why?" Nothing about any of this made sense. *Impossible*

a voice inside her head urged. If only she could believe it. Perhaps if he admitted it to her once, admitted that he experienced this oddly intoxicating attraction as well, they could acknowledge it and put it behind them forever.

His thumb began moving back and forth over the pulse on her wrist. Her breathing hitched. "Why?" He echoed her question. "Because I'm inches from becoming officially betrothed to a lady I can barely stand to sit in the same room with for more than ten minutes. Because I've responsibilities I cannot ignore. But, most of all, because I can no longer ignore the spell you've cast upon me." He remained sitting, but with her diminutive height, her eyes were nearly even with his. "Let me kiss you Charlotte."

Her heart beat so quickly she half expected it to burst from her chest and charge out of the room. She went to answer him, but nothing emerged from her mouth.

"Would you like me to kiss you?"

She should lie. She should deny wanting anything of the sort.

"Yes," she whispered. The one word was all he required.

A gentle tug from him and suddenly she was sitting on the bench again. This time she was between his legs, their faces only inches apart now. "But you shouldn't," she added.

"I'm well aware of that."

And then his hand was at the back of her mob-capped head, pulling her even closer. Charlotte parted her lips and waited.

Oh, yes.

❧

SHE TASTED EXACTLY as he'd imagined she would. Honey. Sweet. Velvety. Warmth. Her lips opened without coaxing, mingling their breath.

Anthony turned his head to access her mouth more easily. An overwhelming... rightness swept through him. Everything about her excited and invigorated him. Yet he felt as though he'd held her like this a million times.

How could he live the entirety of his life without having this, without having her, ever again?

He'd allow himself this moment. "Charlotte," he whispered. Saying her name aloud made all of this more real, somehow. She'd haunted his dreams, tantalized him from a place just out of bounds. But today, in this moment, he'd managed to break through those barriers, eliminate societies boundaries.

"M'lord," her whisper barely reached his hearing over the blood rushing through his veins.

"Anthony." He shouldn't. He oughtn't. But God only knew how much he wanted to hear his name upon her lips.

"Anthony," she whispered. "You must... We. We must stop." She labored to speak the words, but he heeded them against his own inclinations.

Although ending the kiss, he didn't release her person. And she hadn't expected him too. She hadn't relinquished her grip around his neck and her face remained buried against his chest.

She intoxicated him as no spirits ever could.

If this were only about him... He choked on a wave of unexpected emotion.

When he went to press his lips against her hair, his lips landed on the muslin fabric of her cap. Scattering reason and rational thought to the wind, he gripped the material and tugged it off.

She didn't fight it, but instead tilted her head back and met his gaze, catching his breath with her beauty.

White fire, he could see, even braided and pinned up. Not just gold, but yellow and white and amber threaded together. He wanted nothing more than to...

"It's beautiful." But his voice caught. "So beautiful."

"But you cannot," She reminded him. "You have obligations."

He shook his head as though dismissing his duties, his responsibilities, if only for this instant. "I could take care of you. Purchase a cottage nearby. No one need know--"

And then several offkey voices, singing ironically enough the same song Charlotte had sung for him, drifted through the corridor. A group of jovial-sounding guests approached. Staring back at him in horror, Charlotte jumped off the bench as though scalded. She searched around, seized the cap from him, and sprung to the other side of the room.

What had he just done? Had he actually suggested she become his mistress? It was nothing he'd ever considered for himself. And by the look on her face, he'd insulted her in the worst way. She was a damned vicar's daughter, for God's sake! What in the hell had he been thinking?

But she was also alone in this world.

"We can use the pianoforte. Billings plays well enough." Miss Fairchild had opened the door with several of her cousins following behind her. "Ah, Lord Mapleton. I wondered where you'd gone off to." She turned to the three gentlemen and ladies behind her. "You all remember Lord Mapleton, my, er, ahem. Lord Mapleton is Father's favorite neighbor. He's stranded because of this awful storm." She'd barely covered her near slip. Nothing was official yet, after all. And then she caught sight of Charlotte near the window.

"Drake! What are you doing down here, for Heaven's sake?" Charlotte had donned her cap once again and was vigorously polishing a picture frame with her back to the room. "I'm sure Cook can use your assistance preparing supper." Those who'd accompanied his fiancé ignored Charlotte. She was only a servant, after all.

Nausea settled into Anthony's gut as the woman he'd been kissing only minutes before shuffled out of the room at the behest of the woman who was to become his wife.

Charlotte didn't turn back to acknowledge him.

As she shouldn't. Likely she hated him after such an affront.

He ran one hand through his hair and turned to face Miss Fairchild who seemed vibrant and animated now. Lucky girl, she hadn't had to entertain him for all of four hours.

Had it been four hours? He glanced out the window and then to check the large clock by the door. The snow hadn't let up as he'd hoped. In fact, it likely had strengthened. Daphne and Michael would be at home alone with their mother.

On Christmas Eve.

But he'd promised Daphne he wouldn't make the trip, short though it might be, if the weather turned.

And damned if it hadn't turned against him. Much like his heart.

"You missed out on all the fun!" One of Miss Fairchild's cousins, the girl couldn't be older than ten and seven, informed him. "We've been collecting greenery and having snow wars. It's freezing outside! We thought we'd sing carols while the servants hang our cuttings." And then she caught Miss Fairchild's gaze and the two of them giggled.

He felt positively ancient.

He also felt like a villain of the worst kind.

CHAPTER 9

SACKED

As soon as the music room door closed behind her, Charlotte pressed her back against the wall and covered her face with her hands. Hints of lemon oil scented the rag she still clutched, which oddly enough, soothed her.

What had he been offering her? But she knew the answer without having to even think about it. He'd suggested harboring her in secret.

As his mistress.

One moment she'd been caught up in a romantic dream. The way he touched her. His questions about her father... She hadn't imagined his affection.

He'd trembled in her arms.

A groan escaped her lips. Why had he asked her that? Was it only for him? She'd thought he saw her as more than that. She'd suspected that he pitied her, but she'd also thought he... respected her.

The sounds from within reminded her that she could be discovered at any moment. She dropped her hands from her face and found herself staring into very angry eyes.

Lady Denton.

"I don't think I'm wrong that you are not happy at Glenstone Hollow." She narrowed her eyes. "Because you think yourself above your station. Did you think no one would see you sitting in the garden last night with my daughter's intended?"

Charlotte opened her mouth to make some sort of denial or explanation, but no sound emerged.

"My husband hired you as a favor to the Vicar and so I cannot simply sack you. I've an aunt in Scotland, however, who has never been able to retain a steady companion. I believe you might be the perfect person for the position."

Scotland? All sorts of emotions rushed through Charlotte. But before she could examine any of them, the viscountess continued.

"Aunt Constance won't put up with your behavior. You'll mind yourself with her or live to regret it."

"But I don't want to go to Scotland." The words flew out unheeded. Surely, the woman wouldn't expect her to leave everything she knew? "I--"

"I couldn't care less what your inclinations are, young woman. Whether you go to Scotland or all the way to America, it's little matter to me. But I've arranged for you to be gone first thing in the morning. As soon as this blasted storm moves out. Be thankful I'm not a cruel woman, lest you find yourself trekking off my husband's property on foot, and without references."

"Thank you, my lady." Charlotte murmured, stunned at this dizzying change of her circumstances. Her circumstances were becoming all too real. Nothing Charlotte said or did right now could change the fact that she was utterly dependent upon this woman. A woman who would do anything necessary to protect her daughter, and rightly so.

If Lady Denton decided to send her packing tonight, Charlotte was doubtful she could survive.

Without her father's protections, her life held little value to anyone. She'd run out of choices and it was no one's fault but her own.

"You're relieved of your position as of now. I'll have a more experienced servant assist her in dressing for this evening."

Charlotte's heart sunk.

She could not return to her brother's home and yet she had nowhere else to go. But... Scotland?

In that moment she blinked and nodded. "Yes, my lady." She wanted to turn and flee ––find somewhere to hide and allow herself a long pitying cry.

But this was not her home. She resided here only so long as she fulfilled her duties to her employer's expectations.

Which she apparently had not. "Will that be all?" She studied the floor, unwilling to meet Lady Denton's gaze.

"Be prepared to depart at dawn." The woman's voice held no uncertainty.

Charlotte nodded again and then turned to leave.

"Unless you're willing to be his whore." The bitter words landed like a knife between her shoulders.

Charlotte wanted to lash out, but the viscountess was right! Unwilling to listen to anything more without striking back, Charlotte burst into a run, nearly sliding and falling on her face in the process.

She hated this place! She hated Lady Denton! And Susan! And... him!

Most of all she hated him!

Once in the dressing room that had been her only private space, breathless and distraught, Charlotte drew out her carpet bag and stuffed her meager belongings in without bothering to fold them. She had her scarf and coat. Her torn gloves and two dull muslin dresses. She'd not bring the horrid mob cap.

Her journal. The watch her father had worn every day.

And nothing else.

She had no money.

Nowhere to go.

The storm raging within her rivaled the blizzard outside. To depart on her own at night, in freezing and wet weather, would mean certain death. She glanced down at her pathetic belongings and sighed. She needed to cut all ties with Lady Denton and her daughter, the future Lady Mapleton.

She needed to be certain never to see him again.

Because the explosive, powerful emotions that somehow sparked between the two of them could not be put to the test again. Had they not been interrupted in the music room she could not be certain she would not have abandoned all sense. As it was, she'd practically thrown herself at him.

He'd removed some of the pins from her hair.

And then he'd offered her that horrid proposal! Which, if she were to be honest with herself, ought not to have come as a surprise.

But it had been in the heat of the moment.

He wasn't the sort of man to marry one woman and keep a mistress on the side. Was he? Despite his suggestion, he was a man of honor. She didn't know how, or why, but she knew this about him. He'd made the offer on impulse, spurred by the passion of their embrace.

And she was not a woman who could give herself to another woman's husband. She'd been raised a vicar's daughter, and her father's teachings remained in her heart.

But Lord Mapleton's offer had been tempting…

Anthony.

She shook her head, dismissing the memory of his need to hear her speak his name.

"Miss Drake?" The housekeeper's voice called out. After spending hours polishing silverware while listening to the woman regale her with all the village gossip, Charlotte would know that woman's voice in her sleep.

Charlotte wiped her eyes and stuffed her bag into the back of the closet and then she emerged, ready to tackle whatever task awaited.

"Do you have need of me, Mrs. Gibson?"

But the housekeeper was already shaking her head. "This arrived yesterday. I've been so busy that I forgot to give it to you." Her eyes were filled with pity. She knew.

"Did Lady Denton speak with you then?"

Mrs. Gibson nodded. "I'm sorry to see you go. I think you would have eventually made a fine companion." But then she laughed. "With a little time and a lot of help."

And then the older woman held out an envelope.

"When you're finished, her ladyship says you're to help out in the kitchen."

Charlotte nodded vaguely. The envelope sent all kinds of thoughts racing through her mind. "I'll be right there," she mumbled.

Mrs. Gibson brushed her hands on her apron and then took her leave.

As soon as the door closed behind her, Charlotte tore open the missive. She read through the hastily scrawled lines three times before convincing herself of their meaning. Perhaps there was somewhere she could go after all...

⁓

ANTHONY DIDN'T STAY with the group of revelers for long. Sick with himself, and not from merely the liquor he'd consumed earlier, he located the chamber Lady Denton had had prepared for him but doubted he'd get any rest.

Reaching into his jacket, he removed the package he'd been carrying around all day. He should have given it to her when he had the opportunity. It was nothing, he knew, but...

His own horrid words haunted him: *I could take care of you. Purchase a cottage nearby. No one need know.*

He'd been caught up in everything about her, fearful of losing her forever. But that didn't excuse the disgusting offer.

He *loved her.* It shouldn't be possible but it was true just the same.

He rewrapped the gift and placed it on the single bureau by the window. Pacing across the room at least ten times, he fought the urge to seek her out. The thought that she hated him, that she believed he thought so little of her was nearly too much to bear.

It haunted him already.

And yet he did not require her forgiveness. In fact, she'd be better off hating him.

The distant gong announcing supper interrupted his thoughts. Lord Denton would be present tonight. Would the viscount expect them to discuss marriage contracts? Anthony threw back the drapes. Darkness had fallen and the moon shone brightly. Of course, now, the storm would let up.

He wondered if Daphne and Michael were sitting down to eat in their mother's chamber. Every year, without fail, his father, and then he and Michael had procured the traditional Yule Log. They'd light it on Christmas Eve in anticipation of the celebrations the following day.

Anthony had been looking forward to renewing the tradition of a large community gathering on Christmas day. His mother hadn't been up to it after his father's passing, and since then he'd not had the heart to undertake the planning himself.

He wanted the celebration. He wanted a family.

He could not marry Miss Fairchild.

An impressive dowry could never replace contentment. Peace. Joy. He'd have to find some other way to meet all of his responsibilities. Air filled his lungs. He'd sell everything he owned that was not entailed but he would not sell himself.

All the money in the world couldn't replace being with the one person who loved you more than anyone else. It couldn't replace climbing into bed each night knowing he wouldn't wake up alone.

It could not replace the knowledge that he was able to protect the woman he loved, able to provide for her, watch her grow large with his child.

He would not discuss marriage contracts with Lord Denton tonight.

The sky beckoned with twinkling stars and a bright

moon. He could travel the short distance to be with his family. He would tell them of his decision tonight.

And then tomorrow, he would return and break things off with Miss Fairchild. Somehow, he did not think the young woman would be overly disappointed.

Only then, could he speak with Charlotte.

CHAPTER 10

HOPE

After spilling the entire contents of a pot onto the floor, one that had been simmering all day, and then knocking a pie off the table in her efforts to assist one of the footmen, Charlotte found herself being banished from the kitchen by the harried cook.

When God created Christmastime, he'd obviously forgotten to make provisions for the servants to celebrate as well. Because after all the food had been served and the drinks consumed, there would be cleaning and scrubbing to prepare for the large party scheduled for the following evening.

Christmastime, she decided in that moment, was for the wealthy and entitled.

Feeling tired and useless, she dismissed such a dismal opinion.

She'd received the gift of a sliver of hope. Her mother's aunt had only recently learned that she was orphaned. She offered her a home and said she'd be interested in presenting her to society in London. She'd told her she need not ever worry. Charlotte would not be without a roof over her head.

She would not be the companion to a cruel old woman in Scotland.

Charlotte shuffled through the corridor toward Miss Fairchild's chamber. Another maid had already taken over her duties, but Charlotte had nowhere else to sleep. Charlotte no longer believed in fate, or destiny. But with this new opportunity, she almost believed in good luck.

The guests would be dining now, celebrating the eve of their savior's birth. With roast beef, duck, potatoes, squash, brussels sprouts and Christmas pudding.

She stifled an ironic chuckle. There would be no turtle soup, however, nor would there be any pie. Oh, but her arms ached. One would have thought she'd been stirring pots all day long. She closed her eyes, rolled her shoulders, and––

Went crashing into something tall, and solid.

"My lord." She gulped as she stared into Lord Mapleton's eyes.

He was dressed in his great coat, had a scarf wound around his throat and had donned his gloves. "Why are you not taking supper with the other guests? You're leaving?" How preposterous for her to demand any sort of explanation from him!

She'd convinced herself she'd never see him again.

Part of her rejoiced at this last opportunity to drink him in. Another part wept at the cruelty of it.

His eyes shown, however, with an excitement she'd not seen in them before. "The storm has let up and I wish to spend Christmas Eve with my family." But he had grasped her by the shoulders.

He seemed lighter in spirit, somehow. She caught her breath when, with all his attention upon her, he smiled. Not the rueful grin she'd witnessed before, but an expression of hope.

He reached inside his coat, searched around and then presented her with a carefully wrapped package tied with a red bow. "Wait until morning to open it."

A gift? He'd purchased her a gift!

Without taking the package from him, she unclasped the scissors from the sewing chatelaine at her waist. She reached beneath her cap and snipped a lock of hair. Unclasping the chain she always wore, she then drew out the locket and secured the hair inside.

He didn't stop her nor ask what she was doing, just waited until she'd held out her token to him. Only then would she take his gift.

Which was the height of impropriety, but she did not care. She would have something to remember him by.

This was goodbye. She glanced up at the ceiling, hoping… But no.

Where was mistletoe when a girl needed it?

And then the lack of greenery hanging above them was no longer a problem. His mouth landed on hers for the most urgent of kisses. How was it that his lips could be hard and demanding but at the same time, soft and coaxing? She didn't know. She only felt.

Oh, Anthony.

Oh, my love.

Her knees went weak by the time he saw fit to release her.

"Will you forgive me?" Emotion strained his voice. "Forgive my rash words earlier today. I did not mean any offence. I got… carried away and--"

She covered his lips with one finger.

"All is forgiven." She'd known it. His character had never been in question.

His gaze locked with hers and he nodded. He did not push her hand away, but mumbled beneath her touch. "Thank you."

She studied the creases by his eyes, the way his hair swept away from his face, but for one wayward lock. And the strength of his cheeks, and chin. His nose wasn't quite perfect. And his lips. Those lips she'd crave… She must memorize his features to draw upon for the remainder of her life.

"Merry Christmas, Charlotte." He grinned.

Dear God, but he must have reconciled himself to his betrothal. Her left side, just above her breast, ached. Her eyes stung but she forced herself to smile.

"Merry Christmas… Anthony."

He leaned forward to press his mouth against hers one last time. Without thought, her arms snaked up to wind around his neck. She had to stand on her toes to reach him but was not to be deterred. Panic had struck her without warning.

She could not allow him to go.

Not yet.

Parting her lips, she tasted his. And then his mouth opened, and the kiss deepened. His hard body pressed against hers from shoulders to just below her thighs. He wanted her, she knew. Perhaps that was all this ever was.

Nonetheless, she was a woman drowning, clinging to a sinking raft.

When he finally pulled away, he rested his forehead against hers. "We'll speak tomorrow."

She nodded. Had she just made a fool of herself? But he held her against him, still. She would be miles away by the time he remembered to seek her out. She wanted to tell him goodbye. She wanted to tell him that she loved him.

He released her and took three steps backward.

"Anthony!" She halted him one last time.

He tilted his head.

"I–I..." She could not do it. "Merry Christmas."

And with one last smile, he was gone.

"TELL me you did not travel in this weather! In the dark, no less!" Daphne set her knitting aside as Anthony carried in the log he'd chosen for this year's Yule, Rufus and Walter trailing behind him. He grinned, feeling more invigorated than he had all week.

He and his driver had borrowed a sleigh from Lord Denton, promising to return it tomorrow. "It's like daylight out there. Did you start the fire with the piece cut from last year's log?"

His sister shook her head, as though in a daze. "I didn't think you'd be coming and didn't want bad luck... What has come over you? I take it you've resolved the marriage contracts then?"

Michael, who'd been snoring softly on the settee, roused himself. Likely hearing the word 'marriage' was enough to disturb his dreams. "What? You're back! And you don't look as though your dog just died, as you did this morning before leaving."

Anthony placed the log on the floor near the hearth and then turned to face these two. They would be affected by his decision. He jammed his hands into his pockets and then lifted his chin. "I've decided against the betrothal."

"Thank God." Both Michael and Daphne responded at once.

"I'm so glad!"

"What did Miss Fairchild say? Oh, Heavens! And the Viscountess!"

Anthony winced. "I haven't told either yet."

Michael laughed and Daphne groaned.

"When do you plan to have this discussion?" Daphne's forehead wrinkled. "Surely not–"

"Tomorrow." Anthony would be totally upfront with them. "But there is more."

This time his younger siblings remained mute, simply waiting for him to continue.

"I'm going to ask another lady." If possible, the room fell even quieter. Not even the logs in the fire dared make any popping sounds. "Miss Charlotte Drake."

"You rogue you." Michael stared at him with admiration in his gaze. "Who is she? Someone you met in London last spring?"

But Daphne's eyes had narrowed. "Miss Drake? Surely not." She sputtered. "Drake? Miss Fairchild's *companion*?"

Anthony nodded. "She is Miss Charlotte Drake." And he loved her. And he believed she loved him back. "She is a vicar's daughter, fallen on hard times. She is refined, plays the piano beautifully. Educated. Sweet. Charming." She'd kissed him as though he were saying goodbye forever. He planned on surprising her tomorrow. He'd drop onto one knee. "I want to give her grandmother's ring."

Daphne, as usual, watched him carefully. "You... love her?"

He dug in his heels. "I don't give a damn who her family is. I could care less about what the ton has to say about all of this." He'd marry her. "If she'll have me. God, I hope she'll have me.

"The trouble is..." he continued. "Without Miss Fairchild's dowry, finances will be tight–considerably so–over the next few years. I'll have to cut your allowance nearly by half," Anthony winced in his brother's direction. "And Daph, we'll need to delay your season by a year or two..."

Daphne rose from her chair and paced across the room. "None of that matters if she is the right bride for you. Don't get me wrong, Anth." She spoke in levelled tones. "I want your happiness more than anything else. My only concern is that you are not being led on a merry chase. What if she is only using you? You're a titled gentleman, wealthy enough in your own right. Likely something of a king to the likes of her."

"She's done nothing of the sort. She's done her best to avoid me, in fact."

"Have you thought of taking her on in a less permanent capacity? Are you certain you need to marry the chit?" Michael's eyes flicked toward Daphne. "Sorry, sis."

Michael's words were far less crass than his own had been and still, Anthony cringed at them. "That is the last time you'll say anything of the kind in my hearing." His voice came out gruffer than he'd intended.

"Just checking." But then his younger brother rose and crossed the room with an outstretched hand. "I'm happy for you." They gripped hands, but then Anthony couldn't help but clasp his brother in a brief, and quite manly, embrace.

His siblings were all he'd had since their father's passing. Daphne joined them, her eyes shinier than normal. When they all separated, feeling more blessed than embarrassed, Anthony brushed his hands together. "Let's get this Christmas Eve celebration underway."

THE NEXT MORNING, feeling considerably less confident than he had the night before, Anthony rode the sleigh back to his neighbor's estate. The Viscount would expect to speak with him first. Anthony would like to be allowed a private word, alone, with Miss Fairchild. Dash it all but he'd done naught but stir up something of a hornet's nest.

It would be worth it though. He hoped.

He would see Charlotte again today.

His heart nearly thumped out of his chest at the thought.

Once inside, the butler asked him to wait in the same room he'd been delegated to the previous morning. Ten minutes passed. Then fifteen. He wondered if his absence from Christmas Eve dinner hadn't gone over all that well.

After cooling his heels for thirty minutes, the door opened, but it was not the viscount. Rather, the Viscountess and Miss Fairchild.

Lady Denton's demeanor was cool, and the younger girl sent him a worried look.

"I understand you requested a word with my husband," The Viscountess began. "He's yet abed but if… necessary. I can persuade him to rise."

Anthony cleared his throat. This was not any meeting he'd ever wished to have. "Would it be possible to have a word with your daughter?" He cleared his throat again. "Alone?"

The older woman glanced between him and Miss Fairchild with pinched lips.

"It's all right, Mama." Miss Fairchild spoke softly, and then demurely sat down.

"I'll be leaving the door ajar." Lady Denton rose, albeit reluctantly, and strode from the room. As promised, she left the door open by at least twelve inches.

Miss Fairchild looked up at him as he'd remained on his feet. "Won't you sit down?"

Taking a deep breath, Anthony lowered himself to the chair directly across from her.

"I don't suppose you've come to wish me Merry Christmas." She gave him a wry smile. "Since you left last night, without speaking to Father, I'd guess you are either here to confirm my consent before speaking to him again... Or something else altogether."

He refused to clear his throat again. Twisting his face into a somber expression he took a deep breath. "I am here, with abject apologies, Miss Fairchild. For I fear you and I wouldn't suit–"

Miss Fairchild interjected. "I rescind my agreement to your proposal, my lord. Since nothing has been made public, I feel I'm not acting improperly by telling you this."

"Not at all." And yet he needed to run her words through his mind again in order to fully comprehend her meaning. Thank God, he'd dodged that bullet. "Have you told anyone?"

She shook her head. Brown curls remaining surprisingly still. "No one except for Drake, my maid. And since mother sent her packing, I needn't worry about her telling anyone."

Anthony let out a breath of relief. She'd only told Drake.

Her maid.

Charlotte. *Her mother had what?*

"Excuse me? Your mother sent Miss Drake where?" A huge lump formed in his throat. "On Christmas?"

Miss Fairchild shrugged. "She was a poor companion and equally inept at being a lady's maid."

She cannot have gone far. He'd just spoken with her last night!

"Do you know where she went?" He knew he shouldn't be asking Miss Fairchild this, but it was possible Charlotte had told her where she would go.

"Mama says Scotland. I have an aunt who requires a companion." Miss Fairchild shuttered. "A veritable demon, that woman. I must admit, I don't envy Drake such an appointment." And then a pretty sigh. "She should have tried harder at her position here."

Anthony burst from the chair, knocking it over in the process. She cannot have travelled far in these conditions. A good deal of the snow was already melted but the roads remained muddy and wet. Panic struck at the thought of how vulnerable she would be.

Before he could excuse himself, the viscountess pushed the door opened. "Is everything all right in here?"

Just the person who might hold the answers he needed. As much as he hated revealing too much of his personal inclinations to Lady Denton, his need to locate Charlotte was even greater.

"Your daughter says Miss Drake, has left your employ."

A satisfied look entered the lady's eyes. "She has. I dismissed her yesterday afternoon. Was there any particular reason, my lord, that you would be inquiring as to one of our former employee's current situation?"

In that instant, he knew. Charlotte lost her job because of him.

Yesterday afternoon. She'd known when she saw him last night. Damn his eyes, he should have told her of his plans then. He shouldn't have left anything to chance.

She *had* been telling him goodbye forever. He slipped his hand into the pocket where he carried her locket and grasped it in his palm.

"I wish to speak with the lady. When did she leave?"

Lady Denton flicked some imaginary lent from the sleeve of her dress. "Hours ago."

"Scotland?"

Another long drawn out pause. "She refused my offer. Foolish girl. If she thinks she's going to get a reference from me, then she has another thing coming."

He'd have to strangle this woman before she'd give him the information he needed. With a nod in Miss Fairchild's direction, Anthony practically sprinted from the room.

What had Daphne told him when he'd first met Charlotte? It had been the vicar who had recommended her to Denton in the first place. He'd have no difficulty finding the vicar. On Christmas morning, he'd be either at home or the church, preparing for services. Wouldn't he?

What in the hell did a vicar do when he wasn't preaching from the pulpit anyhow?

He'd damned well be finding out soon enough. He glanced toward Viscount Denton's closed door. He and the man had had a good relationship for as long as he'd remembered. He'd have to make amends another time.

All he could think of right now was locating Charlotte.

CHAPTER 11

CHRISTMAS DAY

"Amen." Charlotte spoke the word, oh so gratefully.

She'd asked the driver to deliver her to the vicarage this morning instead of Scotland. Kenneth had not complained. Bundled from head to toe, he'd been only too grateful to cancel such a dangerous journey in the midst of winter. As it was, even the short drive to the vicarage took longer than normal.

This was the only place she could think to come today where she wouldn't be turned away. Mr. Frye the local vicar, had been a friend of her father's. He was also a man of God.

As luck would have it, Charlotte was not to be destitute after all. But until she could make the journey to meet her aunt, she was grateful for a roof over her head. Mrs. Gibson had given her a shilling when she'd left. Charlotte hadn't wanted to take it, suspecting it came from the housekeeper's own pocket, but she hadn't much choice if she were to make it to London.

Lady Denton had not mentioned Charlotte's wages when she'd dismissed her.

Hopefully Charlotte could repay the housekeeper someday soon.

If only she could make the journey on foot. That would be foolish though. She needed to be patient. The mail coaches were notorious for running on time but wouldn't be operating on Christmas day. She wasn't keen to travel over muddy roads, anyhow and she was, oh, so grateful to be out of the cold.

The vicar and his sister had welcomed her with open arms when she'd arrived just after sun up. She'd stood on their doorstep with nothing but her bag, wearing her well-worn coat, her scarf and the loveliest pair of gloves she'd ever hoped to own.

She'd opened his present as soon as she'd settled onto her cot the night before.

And then she'd cried her eyes out.

"It's a shame that things didn't work out for you up there," Mr. Frye commented as he served himself a portion of potatoes. A fire crackled in the hearth. Not only had they taken her in, but now they would share their Christmas dinner with her.

"I don't blame her a bit." Miss Frye, a heavyset woman of about fifty or so, slid Charlotte a sideways glance. "Mildred Hanover said Lady Denton didn't pay her bill last month because the delivery didn't come on the day she wanted it. All of three pounds! Her husband owns the mercantile," she explained to Charlotte. "I certainly wouldn't wish to be in that woman's employ."

"Be that as it may, Miss Drake is going to need to learn to deal with these sorts, learn to humble herself. Employment doesn't come easy and now she's got herself into something of a jam. Not that we won't put you up until the weather's clear enough to travel to your brother's home." The older gentleman lowered his spectacles to stare hard at Charlotte. "Your father would have done the same for any child of mine. Especially on Christmas day."

"And I appreciate it, Sir." The tumult of emotions Charlotte felt had stolen her appetite for the day, but she tore off a piece of homemade bread, nonetheless. She'd never been heartbroken before and hoped never to be so again.

Nervousness attacked as well.

Borrowing ink and pen from Susan's lap desk, Charlotte had penned a response to her aunt's letter immediately, but after the events of the day before, being sacked and all, she'd decided to simply deliver it herself.

Meanwhile, she needed to endure one more day in Bridges End.

Susan will find a way to make him happy. For his sake, she hoped so. And of course, he'd have the funds he needed to take care of all his obligations. He could continue with the necessary repairs from the fire and on his own estate. He could do what he wished with that blasted canal system. She hoped they were worth it.

It came back to his honor. He would not allow others to suffer so that he could please only himself with his choice of bride.

He would act dutifully and marry a lady of good rank, one of his own.

Charlotte blinked away the stinging at the back of her eyes.

Miss Fairchild would *not* make him happy. It ought to

have given her some consolation, but it did not. She loved him. She wished him happy, of course she did.

And she would be happy again too.

Eventually.

But for now, she needed to endure this heartache. Because fate, or God, or destiny––whoever had created she and Lord Mapleton for one another––had made an awful mistake!

As ANTHONY WENT in search of his driver, one of Denton's older coaches rambled up the drive through the melting snow. It seemed odd to him that the vehicle had gone out to begin with.

"Merry Christmas!" The driver greeted him as he drew the vehicle to a halt outside the stableblock.

Anthony scratched his chin. "Merry Christmas. Have you travelled far today?"

"Not as far as I'd expected, my lord." The driver laughed. "I'm to be home for Christmas after all."

"Where had you expected to travel?" Was it possible…?

"Scotland."

Hope, worry and excitement hit Anthony in one fell swoop. "What have you done with Miss Drake then?"

The servant hopped off from his perch and then brushed his hands together with a good deal of satisfaction. "Lady Denton had me drop her at the vicarage. A shame she won't be around anymore. Prettiest lady below stairs we've had 'ere in ages." And then realizing who he was speaking to, he lowered his gaze. "Pardon my saying so, milord."

But Anthony stopped listening after hearing that Charlotte was not, in fact, trudging through the snow alone. Luckily, John stepped out of the stable in that moment.

"Is the carriage readied?"

"Just now, my lord. You're prepared to leave for Maplehurst?"

"Not just yet. We'll be visiting the vicar this fine afternoon."

John raised his brows but made no comment.

Charlotte could be found only a few miles away.

Anthony calmed his racing heart and climbed up beside his driver. He would have gone to Scotland after her, if necessary. He'd have tracked her to the ends of the earth.

"Ever been in love, John?" The efficient man glanced at him sideways. Of course, Anthony wasn't one to have personal conversations with his employees. He hadn't been in the past, anyhow.

"Only once." John responded.

Love wasn't something Anthony had sought. He'd dreamt of a loving family, of shared holidays filled with laughter and joy, but he'd not realized how much love for his wife was built into that vision.

Until he'd met Charlotte.

"I never believed much in love myself. Was it worth it?"

John grimaced but nodded nonetheless. "Marrying my wife was the best decision I ever made. I'm only happy she accepted me. I wouldn't have blamed her for turning me down, with what little I had to offer her."

Nerves struck Anthony. Would Charlotte have him? Of course, she would.

Wouldn't she?

But what if she refused?

"Not that it's any of my business," John inserted. "But I thought you decided not to marry Miss Fairchild."

"You thought right." Anthony responded. He surprised himself then, by announcing. "Damn fool that I am, I've fallen in love with her companion."

"Miss Drake? Hell, I think we've all fallen a little bit in love with that one."

And again, doubt assaulted him. Anthony apparently wasn't the only man to notice her.

Was it possible she might not love him back?

Was it possible he'd find her, make his offer and then be refused? But no. He couldn't believe that. Her gaze last night had held nothing but love. Of course, she'd marry him!

Wouldn't she?

The few miles they needed to cover passed slowly but Lord Mapleton, Earl and Peer, failed to appreciate the picturesque winter scenery. Instead he began rehearsing the speech he'd make when he saw her again.

He'd damn well have to nail this proposal.

CHAPTER 12

THE PROPOSAL

Anthony was jolted out of his mental preparations when the coach drew to a halt at the tidy little vicarage. He sat up straight, tugged at the collar beneath his greatcoat, and then took a deep breath. "Wish me luck?"

John laughed beside him. "I doubt you'll be needing any of that. You're Mapleton, after all. What servant girl wouldn't jump at the chance at becoming a lady?"

But Anthony knew what servant girl might not jump: Miss Charlotte Drake. Given, she hadn't taken to performing the duties of a companion, but she hadn't been willing to become a kept woman in order to be free of them.

She'd said she had forgiven him for the insult, but what if she had not?

He jumped off the driver's box and landed easily on an area of packed snow. In the same instant, the front door opened, and Miss Frye peaked outside.

"Why, Lord Mapleton, to what do we owe the pleasure of a visit on Christmas day? My brother's finishing up the notes for his Christmas sermon right now but I'm certain he'll be willing to take a break to meet with you. Come in, my lord. You must be chilled to the bone."

Anthony cleared his throat. "Is Miss Drake here?"

The vicar's sister paused and then raised her brows to the very top of her forehead. "Why yes, as a matter of fact, she came to us this morning." And then she studied him with narrowed eyes. "My brother was well acquainted with the young lady's father. God rest his soul."

Yes. Yes. He'd known that. Perhaps... "Would it be possible to have a word with the vicar?" He could not speak with her father, and he had no idea how to contact her brother. Was it possible that the vicar would be willing to give him permission to offer for the young lady?

Circumstances were less than ideal; he'd be the first to admit. But that didn't mean he couldn't do his best to bring some level of propriety to this affair.

"Most certainly, my lord." She took his coat and scarf and then led him into a nearby parlor, notably unoccupied, before disappearing to find her brother.

Charlotte was here.

Had she sat in this same parlor this morning? The vicar's sister hadn't held back in her Christmas decorations. Holly, ribbons, and mistletoe dressings happily declared the joy of the holiday. He hoped he'd have something to celebrate as well.

Would Miss Fryge be informing her of his arrival? Anthony went to tug at his cravat and realized he'd already loosened it considerably. His life, his happiness, hung in the balance today.

If she said no, he'd be devastated. He'd be ruined for all other women. At some point he'd go on to find a bride--not Miss Fairchild--but some other debutante. He'd always know that the woman who was his other half had gotten away, but he would go on to find some sort of peace and contentment.

Eventually.

He hoped he didn't have to find out.

"Mapleton." Dressed all in black, wearing his cleric's collar, the vicar Anthony had known for as long as he could remember, strode into the room, hand outstretched. "Merry Christmas, my lord. What brings you to the vicarage today?"

Anthony cleared his throat. He'd been doing an awful lot of that this week. "I understand Miss Drake is here." He'd not beat around the proverbial bush. "I'm here to ask for her hand and thought, without her father to go to, that you might be willing to stand in his place?"

The serious-minded man nodded sagely. "Sit down, my boy."

Without warning, the words pierced something in Anthony's heart. He'd not been called a boy by anyone, anyone at all, since his father's passing.

Anthony lowered himself onto the worn settee.

"I'll not condescend to ask if you've given the notion a good deal of thought. Is this the actual reason her employment at Glenstone Hollow was terminated?"

"I believe so, sir. I didn't intend–" His throat filled with that something annoying that had plagued him all day. "I feel horrid that Lady Denton saw through me." He'd admit the truth to this man.

Mr. Frye nodded once again. "Is that the reason you are here? Do you feel guilty that Miss Drake has lost her position?"

Anthony was shaking his head before the vicar could

finish his question. "Not at all, sir." And then he decided to make his position as clear as he possibly could. "I've fallen in love with her. I was prepared to betroth myself to Miss Fairchild but when all was said and done, I could not see myself going on without her--without Charlotte, Miss Drake. I realize the situation is not ideal, sir, but I've talked with my brother and sister and they support my decision."

For the first time since walking into the room, the vicar cracked a smile. "Well, then, I imagine you'd like to ask the lady herself. If you don't mind waiting, I'll have my sister fetch the gel." He rose with a grimace and then reached out to shake Anthony's hand. "Her father, I believe would approve. As do I."

CHARLOTTE SMOOTHED her dress as she peered into the small looking glass. She was to attend church with Miss Frye. As this was to be the Christmas day service, *he* would most definitely be in attendance. Likely with Miss Fairchild at his side.

"Miss Drake?" The vicar's kind sister peeked around the door. "There is a guest here to see you." And then the lady, unable to contain a pleased smile, flushed a very bright pink. "Lord Mapleton has had a word with my brother, and now wishes to have a word with you."

But how? Why?

"The *Earl* of Mapleton?" Anthony was the only Lord Mapleton in the district, of course, and yet she felt the need for clarification.

"Yes, dearie." Miss Frye giggled.

"In the parlor?" Charlotte bit her lip. Miss Frye was

acting as though he'd come to ask for her, which of course was ridiculous. And yet.

It was Christmas.

But she'd already been granted two miracles: the letter telling her about her great aunt, and then a place to stay until she could travel.

It would be greedy to wish for one more.

And then a horrid thought crossed her mind. Anthony may have come to renew his initial offer, of which she'd...

Of course, she'd decline it. And then hate him forever after.

"Do you require a moment to compose yourself? Although, he is an earl..."

"No. I'm ready to meet with him." Charlotte didn't want to wait. She wanted to know what he had to say as soon as possible.

She also craved his company desperately.

She took one last glance in the mirror and then followed Miss Frye downstairs.

ANTHONY DIDN'T SEE her immediately. He held his shoulders rigidly, standing at the window and staring outside.

Miss Frye softly pulled the door closed behind Charlotte.

"Merry Christmas, my lord."

He didn't move. "You weren't going to tell me goodbye." And then he turned to gaze at her with those warm, albeit slightly wounded eyes.

And again, she experienced all of those sensations of...

belonging with him. She managed a pained smile. "It was all so hopeless…"

But he was shaking his head. And then covering the steps between them to grasp her hands. "Not hopeless," he stated confidently.

Oh, no. Please do not ask me to be your mistress!

"But it is!" She tore her hands away from him. "I can't ever. My father would roll over in his grave! I'm not… I could never--" This time it was she who turned her back on him.

"Marry me, Charlotte."

She froze. And then forced herself to take three deep breaths. Had he somehow discovered her news? Surely, Mr. Frye would not have said anything regarding her personal circumstances.

"I don't care that you are penniless. I don't care that you were a servant when I first laid eyes upon you. I've spoken to my sister and brother about you, and they don't care about a dowry or family connections. They care only that I am happy. Look at me, Charlotte?" His question sounding almost like a plea.

He wanted to marry her? Even thinking she was nothing more than a servant?

She turned and stared into his face, noticing that his golden-brown hair looked as though he'd ran his hand through it several times and his cravat was loosened even more than it had been all week. Dark circles etched beneath his eyes and he looked as though he hadn't slept at all.

She'd noticed similar shadows beneath her own eyes earlier.

"And what will make you happy, Anthony? Will you be happy when the neighbors' gossip about your common wife? Will you be happy when your account dwindles away and you're not able to repair a manor house that has been in your family for generations? When you are unable to meet your responsibilities?"

He nodded without any hesitation whatsoever.

She wanted him. God knew she wanted to marry him. But not because he pitied her, or merely desired her sexually.

"Why do you want to marry me?"

He closed his eyes for all of a second and then dropped onto one knee. And again, he grasped her hands in his. "Because although we've barely just met, in the deepest part of my heart, I love you. I know it sounds foolish, but you are the other half of me–– the *better half* of me. When I tried to imagine a life without you it was empty and cold. Nothing matters without you by my side. Put me out of my misery, my love, my dear Charlotte, and say you'll be my wife."

Looking down at him, his head bent and his lips pressed against her wrists, she realized that no mistake had been made. He'd felt it too, that magical connection. Her bottom lip began trembling and her knees turned to jelly.

"Yes." She spoke to the top of his head. "Yes, Anthony. I'll marry you."

His head jerked up and for the first time since she'd entered the room, he smiled. "Thank God." He burst to his feet and drew her into the strength of his embrace. "You'll never have to deal with the likes of Lady Denton again."

He leaned back and gazed into her eyes. "You've always been a lady to me. Even when I thought you were a maid, you impressed me with your person. Beautiful, you know, but so much more." He bent forward and his lips hovered less than an inch from hers. The warmth of his breath mingled with her own. "Say the words, Charlotte. Tell me I'm not crazy."

"I love you, Anthony." They weren't merely words, but a promise, a state of fact, a natural law. "I love you so much!"

Pressing up on her tiptoes, she closed the distance between them.

Something like coffee, and the spiciest liquor, and something quite undefinable and masculine compelled her to explore his mouth boldly. She wound her arms around his neck, feeling as though she'd finally found her way home.

Her breasts ached for his touch and she craved him... everywhere.

But they were in the vicar's parlor, and likely Mr. Frye and his sister awaited them on the other side of the closed door.

A low growl drifted past his lips when Charlotte broke their kiss.

He simply held her tightly, both of them waiting for their racing hearts to slow. "I would have chased you to Scotland."

"I no longer have need of employment." She tilted her head back to meet his curious gaze.

With a tender tap on her nose, he grinned. "Of course, you don't, minx."

But she was shaking her head. "But you misunderstand." And then she withdrew the letter from the deep pocket in her skirt. "I received this letter from—I believe she is my great aunt. She asked that I come and stay with her. She wants to present me to Society! Can you imagine that?"

Anthony was frowning now, confused as she handed over the missive she must have read a hundred times. After reading the letter over carefully, he stared back at her with a dazed sort of expression.

"Lady *Sterling* is your great aunt?"

Snatching the letter back, Charlotte studied the name. "I couldn't quite make out the name properly. See here, it is signed Katherine Rochester. She…" Charlotte held the letter close to her face. "Regrets horribly that my grandparents disinherited my mother. When she heard of Papa's passing, she felt it was high time to make amends."

"Do you know who she is?"

"My great aunt?" It was Charlotte's turn to be confused.

And then Anthony was shaking his head and laughing. "Not that it matters one iota to me, love, but you've more pedigree than either Susan Fairchild or myself."

Charlotte set her fingertip upon his lips. "But you loved me as a maid."

Anthony reached up to prevent her escape. "Would you have loved me as a footman?"

She'd thought of this already. "At times, I wished that you had been a footman. But I was willing to love you despite your horrid title."

His brows rose at this. "My horrid title?"

And then she smiled boldly. "Don't worry, love. I may be a lady now, but I'll make love to you like a commoner."

And then she kissed him again.

PEEKING through a crack in the door, the vicar's sister turned mischievously to her brother "I knew that mistletoe would come in handy."

The End

IF YOU ENJOYED THIS BOOK, sign up for Annabelle's Newsletter and receive a free download of her Christmas Novella, Hell Hath Frozen over.

Click here for your free novella!

Cocky Earl

Jules and Charley

An American heiress, A dignified Earl,

and one impossible wager.

Cocky Baron

Chase and Bethany

A Secret Crush. Her brother's best friend.

A scandal to rock all scandals

Cocky Mister

Dec. 7, 2020

Stone and Tabetha

An ambitious debutante clashes with a mere Mister.

Mayfair Maiden

Dec. 8, 2020

Peter Spencer's Story!

Spinoff from Lord Love A Lady Series AND The Regency Cocky
Gents written to release with the

12 Days of Christmas: (Book 8)

Turn the page to read the first chapter

Maybridge Falls, England, December, 1823

Dash blinked several times, attempting to clear his vision, as he stared out the large, square window at the front of the tiny inn. Before him lay a sea of white snow. In fact, the offending precipitation had piled so high he wasn't certain if all the liquor had blinded him, turning his eyesight white, or if there actually was that much powder piled on the ground. At this rate, they'd be stuck in this haven of wholesomeness until spring.

He slowly and methodically refocused his gaze on the fire crackling merrily in the hearth as a way to test his eyes. Snorting, he took another long swig of his ale. Only, the fire was not merry at all. That must be his imagination playing tricks on him.

Clearly, he'd allowed this quaint little village to poison his normally debaucherous mind. It was nearly Christmastide, not that he gave a wit about the holiday. But he and his companions had been on their way to a lovely little affair being put on by a very eligible widow who'd been married to a man five and twenty years her senior. Finding herself suddenly free of attachment, she'd invited Dash, along with a few of his friends, to celebrate the holiday.

Jack had already fallen asleep sitting at the table, his face resting on his plate. Nick was still awake, but barely. Their carriage, unable to continue the journey, had stopped here to wait out the storm. The men had amended to drink themselves into a stupor to pass the time until they could continue on their journey. Nick's head slumped forward, falling on the table with a decided thump. Dash chuckled and pushed Nick's shoulder. "You're a marquess for Christ's sake, you should be able to hold your liquor better than that."

Nick mumbled an incoherent response and then let out a decided snore, making Dash chuckle and he poked his friend again. He missed the man's shoulder, his finger landing in Nick's ear. The man didn't stir.

Clutching at his stomach, Dash laughed all the more and then grabbed a slice of bread from his near-empty plate of meat pie and beans, pulling a crust off and tossing it at Jack. While he'd been aiming for Jack's mouth, the bread lodged firmly in the man's hair.

The sight was so hilarious, a fit of laughter overtook Dash again, and he snorted, tears leaking from his eyes as he pounded the table with his fist. Then he sobered, attempting to sit up straighter. He only ever giggled like this when he was ape-faced drunk.

Which was a distinct possibility.

Focusing all his concentration on the task, he pushed back from the table, his chair scraping the floor. He started to stand but wobbled and held the edge tighter in search of his balance. Head spinning in a sickening manner, he puffed out his cheeks when bile rose in his throat. Bloody bullocks, he really had done a fine job of getting pissed.

Inching up from his semi crouched position, he managed to stand, the room turning about in the strangest way.

Fresh air. That's what he needed. "I'm going outside, boys," he called to his sleeping friends, pointing his finger toward the window. Unfortunately, he'd chosen the wrong hand and rather pointed to the stairs that surely led to his room. For a moment he considered that plan instead. Head up the stairs and collapse into his bed.

Dash scratched his head and then felt in his pocket for a key. What room was he in anyhow? What floor? He scrubbed his face. Perhaps getting drunk hadn't been the best plan after all.

Nothing to do for it now but take a walk in the fresh, cold winter air and clear his muddled head. That widow who waited at the end of their trip was a buxom sort with lots of supple curves. Some might say she ran a bit heavy but a man *needed* that sort of warmth in this kind of weather. He wished he'd arrived at his destination and was in that bed right now rather than here. In fact, he might rather be anywhere else.

With a loud sigh, he shuffled across the floor and as he opened the door he was forced to grip the handle for dear life. The blast of cold air did clear his thoughts a bit and so he stepped out into the cool night inhaling deeply.

His Hessians came up near to his knees but as he stepped into a drift of snow the damn fluffy stuff came up over the tops, making his knees wet and packing down on the insides of his boots.

Dash bent over to try and clear them out. Even in his

drunken state the snow bit at his bare skin. He jerked them back, tucking them close to his body.

Unfortunately, the sudden movement threw off his already precarious balance and as he straightened, his arms flailed wildly in the air. For all his effort, he spun about, putting more of his weight upon one leg and then the other, before toppling over, and landing in a giant pile of snow.

"Bloody hell," he yelled as the cold, white crusts of hell smashed under his jacket, down his breeches and melted in his boots. His arms lay out by his sides, his feet wide apart as though he'd lain down to create a snow angel.

When he lifted his head to sit up, a wave of dizziness crashed over him like he'd never experienced in his life. Resigned now, he grimaced at the inky black sky, snow falling into his eyes and mouth. He was going to die in the snow, in a sleepy little village a week before Christmastide. Couldn't he have been shot in a duel? Or better still, perished in some woman's bed? This…this was below his station and utterly ridiculous.

NOELLE NIBBLED at the gingerbread she'd saved from dinner and stared out into the dark night and watched the swirling snow. She hadn't been able to fall asleep again and had donned her coat and scarf to sit at the window thinking. If only thinking brought her the answers she sought.

She raised the spicy bread to her lips for another bite and closed her eyes so that she didn't miss a single flavor. It was her favorite and despite everything else that was wrong in her life just then, she would enjoy every mouthwatering bite.

It's what her mother would have wanted her to do. Her mother would have told her to be grateful that she had a warm bed to sleep in along with delicious and filling food in her belly when others lived in lack.

And Noelle was grateful for all she was provided.

But she missed her life before—before her mother died, before her father had fallen into despair and given up on all of them. Noelle swallowed the bite of her cookie that had suddenly lodged in her throat. Because in that moment, although they were just a few feet away, each in their own chambers, Noelle missed her sisters too. Perhaps most of all, she longed to laugh with them, argue with them, listen to them tease one another and all the other things they'd done when their mother had been alive.

Be grateful.

She glanced dispassionately around the chamber Aunt Winifred had made available for her. The bedding was lovely, the furnishings were of a deep rich mahogany, the drapes of a beautiful silk, and yet vivid in her mind was the bedchamber she'd left behind.

She hadn't slept through the night once since their father had sent them away. Her breath fogged the window and for the hundredth time, she rubbed it away with her mittened fist.

This too shall pass, she reminded herself as she blinked away tears. Her aunt was a little batty, but she had kind eyes and seemed to want to do what was best for all of them. Feelings of homesickness would fade. They always did. Noelle simply needed to find a way to get her sisters back to normal.

The snow really was pretty. Her mother would have loved a night such as this.

This storm had moved in only a few hours ago and already had accumulated enough that it was impossible to identify where her aunt's lawn ended and the road began. Having been raised in the country, Noelle found it somewhat of a novelty to live in the center of town, even if her aunt's house was old and outrageously large and somewhat of a curiosity.

She popped the last sweet bite past her lips and peered outside again. She would hardly recognize the town square beneath all this snow if not for the statue erected in the center. It was supposedly made in the likeness of one of the town's founders, hundreds of years before.

And then she blinked and tilted her head.

The statue was…

Moving?

She sat up straight and rubbed at the window again. It wasn't a statue at all, but a man. Oh dear.

Midnight was long past and it was likely already two or three in the morning. What on earth would any sane person be doing outside on a bitter night like tonight? Was he mad?

Noelle narrowed her eyes and focused on the shadowy image as he stumbled and then seemed to sway in the wind. Perhaps he was ill.

Two steps forward and then backward and then…he continued backward until he fell to the ground and disappeared into the snow.

"Get up," she urged in a whisper, feeling an inkling of alarm. Was he dead? Why didn't he raise himself out of the snow?

Nothing. Just the sound of the wind against the window rattling the brittle panes and her own breathing.

"Get up," she urged, louder this time as though he might hear her from inside the house and across the square.

Still. Nothing.

Panic rising, Noelle located her boots and pulled them on over her thick woolen socks before rushing back to the window. She still didn't see him. Had he risen and left or was he yet laying in the snow? Buried alive?

He might never get up if he stayed out there much longer.

Noelle didn't allow herself to reconsider her actions as she tiptoed out of her room and down the front stairs. She was almost surprised to find her aunt's butler absent from the door. Of course, Mr. Clark was in bed. Of course, he was asleep. Normal people slept at this time.

Drawing in a deep breath to fortify her courage, she decided she would help check on him herself. If she couldn't rouse him, then she'd wake the household up.

Finding a dead man in the town center, Noelle supposed, would likely be the sort of event for which a lady might wish to wake a few people.

She unlocked the door and opened it and when the wind blew inside, the cold sent a shiver traveling through her small frame. Undeterred, she clutched the scarf around her head and ducked outside into the dark, wretched storm.

Oh, but the snow was deep, and cold, and wet. Curling her spine against the wind, Noelle kept her head down and barreled headlong in the direction she'd thought she'd seen him fall. What if she couldn't find him?

What if he was a murderer and this was all just a ruse to lure an innocent girl like herself out of her bed chamber and into his clutches?

She did her best to dismiss such pessimistic thoughts

and glanced up to get her bearings, half hoping she would see him and half hoping he'd already made his way back to wherever he'd come from, inside where it was safe and dry.

Both parts of her were to be rewarded, or disappointed, depending on how she cared to think about it, when she caught sight of the dark figure on the ground just a few steps away. Ploughing her way through the snow, she dropped to her knees at his side purposely ignoring the cold now seeping through her coat and night rail. A man's life was at stake, for goodness sake!

"Sir!" She leaned forward to get a better look at him. Even in her panic, in the middle of a blizzard, she couldn't help but notice that he had beautiful, thick, dark lashes. So thick that they'd captured a few sparkling snowflakes and appeared almost magical against the pale skin just above strong cheekbones.

"Sir! Wake up!"

And then her gaze settled on his mouth. Framed with dark stubble above his upper lip and jaw, his lips looked soft but also firm. The word "kissable" flitted through her brain.

She shook her head. Men's lips weren't kissable! Were they?

"Oh please, wake up! Don't be dead!" Not wanting to wake the entire village, she realized she was whispering. She didn't wish to be too loud. It would be dreadfully embarrassing and scandalous if anyone discovered her outside by herself like this.

She removed her gloves and slapped his face a few times as an alternative. He was far too handsome to be dead. "Please!" Her fingers inadvertently threaded themselves through silky, thick, black hair. "You must wake up."

Her fingers continued combing through his hair—strictly to remove the snow, that was.

And then his chest began shaking and she jumped guiltily. Which was ridiculous. She was saving him, for heaven's sake!

"Are you cold?" He must be.

But when that kissable mouth of his stretched into a wide smile, a dreadful feeling rolled through her. He smelled of an all-too-familiar aroma, one she easily recognized as she'd caught the scent on her father's breath often enough.

This blighter was foxed! And he wasn't shaking from cold, he was shaking with laughter now.

Those annoyingly gorgeous lashes of his fluttered and opened to gaze at her sleepily. "Are you an angel, love? Because if you are, I should have died years ago." Hooded and drunken eyes gazed at her as he reached up to touch her face.

Noelle brushed it away and shook him. "You have to get up, sir. You can't stay out here in the cold all night."

"Come down here and join me. We can keep one another warm." His voice sounded low and inviting, sending a deep rumble of delicious sin vibrating through her, despite the freezing snow.

Good Gravy. Jug bitten for certain! "You must get up!" Noelle took hold of his shoulders and made a valiant attempt at pulling him into a sitting position. If his arms hadn't wound about her, she might even have succeeded.

Instead she found herself laying atop the bounder.

"Kiss me first. Kiss me and then I'll do anything you want." He was still staring at her from beneath those damned lashes of his. His body felt warm beneath her despite the wind and snow howling around them.

"Oh, but please?" Noelle pushed herself up so that her face wasn't quite so very close to his. And then her gaze dropped to his lips for an instant. "I really don't want you to die out here."

"One kiss." Those lips of his nearly had her mesmerized. They were so supple and full, curved into the slightest grin.

Perhaps it was due to the late hour. Maybe, it was the hopelessness she'd felt for months now. Or possibly it was simply the fact that her toes were quickly turning into ice but whatever the reason, she was willing to negotiate if it meant getting both of them out of the snow and by a fire.

"You will come with me. If I kiss you?"

"Oh, for certain." He licked his lips and Noelle realized she had licked her own in response.

"Very well." She leaned forward and pressed her mouth against his. And oh, dear. She'd been quite right. They were kissable indeed. Cold but also warm. Soft but also hard. Butterflies took flight in her belly and she thought her heart would burst out of her chest.

But she was a lady and she had a task to complete and pulled away before she allowed herself to do something really stupid—such as allow him to keep on kissing her.

"Now." She spoke firmly as she crawled off of him and back onto her knees. "Get up. You'll feel right horrible for the rest of your life if I fall ill and die simply because you refused to rouse yourself enough so that both of us can get inside, won't you?"

Something in his eyes changed in that moment. Something that led her to believe that he may be something different than the drunken fellow she'd taken him for at first. He might be a guest at the inn, but since she hadn't met many people since coming here, she wouldn't recognize him even if he was one of the local townsmen. He'd grown serious though and no longer looked uncaring and crazed.

He nodded and after a bit of fumbling, grunting, and pulling, she managed to assist him to his feet.

"Where?" He mumbled as he leaned on her heavily. She bit her lip. If he was a guest of the inn, wouldn't he have said so?

"This way," she said, making her decision. He might not belong at the inn and besides that, she'd rather not present herself to a room full of strangers while wearing only her coat and scarf and boots along with her night rail.

It seemed to take forever, almost as though they took two steps backward for every one step forward and when they finally reached the door to her aunt's house, she felt limp with relief.

When she pushed it open, she was grateful to see Mr. Clark standing there awaiting her, dressed in his coat and boots but with a stockinged cap on his head. "I saw you out my window. I was coming out to help you, my lady."

He got on the other side of her gentleman patient and shouldered most of the weight. Getting him across the square had drained her off all warmth and energy. "Go back to bed now. I'll take care of him." He urged her. Her shoulders hunched in relief.

Noelle didn't really want to relinquish her position but as she stepped back, she nearly toppled over, her knees weak. Despite her urge to continue to care for the man, allowing Mr. Clark to take over was probably for the best.

"You won't let him die? He seems to be a decent sort of

gentleman." She flicked her gaze to the man whose life she'd just saved and grimaced. "Despite his current condition."

"I will not allow him to die, Lady Noelle. But you must go back to bed. If anyone outside this house asks, it was I who brought him in. Do you understand?"

She nodded, grateful for his help both in bringing the man inside and protecting her reputation. "Of course. Thank you."

With one last look, Noelle released her hold on the handsome wretch and then scurried up the stairs.

Oh, my. Kissable, indeed!

Click below to keep reading!

My Dashing Duke

STANDALONES

Miss Fortune's First Kiss

A second chance romance novella

between a governess and an Earl

Not Another Nob

Part of the Marriage Maker Series

Cocky Duke

A Regency retelling of Cocky Bastard

In the Cocky Hero Shared World

CONTEMPORARY ROMANCE

BY ANNABELLE ANDERS

Mile High Madness

6 Romance Novellas set in Colorado

Blame it on the altitude!

ABOUT THE AUTHOR

Annabelle Anders began publishing in 2017 and left her day job a year later. Since then, she's published over ten full length Regency Romance novels, with one of them receiving the distinguished RITA nomination in 2019. She writes at her home in the small town of Grand Junction, Colorado with the "help" of her two miniature dachshunds and husband of over thirty years and is happy to have finally found her place in life.

Find info on all of Annabelle's Books and at www.annabelleanders.com

FREE NOVELLA

Sign up to receive Annabelle's Newsletter

and download the Novella:

Hell Hath Frozen Over

For Free!

Sign up at www.annabelleanders.com